LUCK OF THE DRAW

ROCKIN' RODEO SERIES 1

VICKI THARP

ALSO BY VICKI THARP

Lazy S Ranch Series

Cowgirl, Unexpectedly (Lazy S Ranch 1)

Must Love Horses (Lazy S Ranch 2)

Hot on the Trail (Lazy S Ranch 3)

Rockin' Rodeo Series

Luck of the Draw (Rockin' Rodeo 1)

Photo Chute (Rockin' Rodeo 2)

Wright's Island Series

Don't Look Back (Wright's Island 1)

In Her Defense (Wright's Island 2)

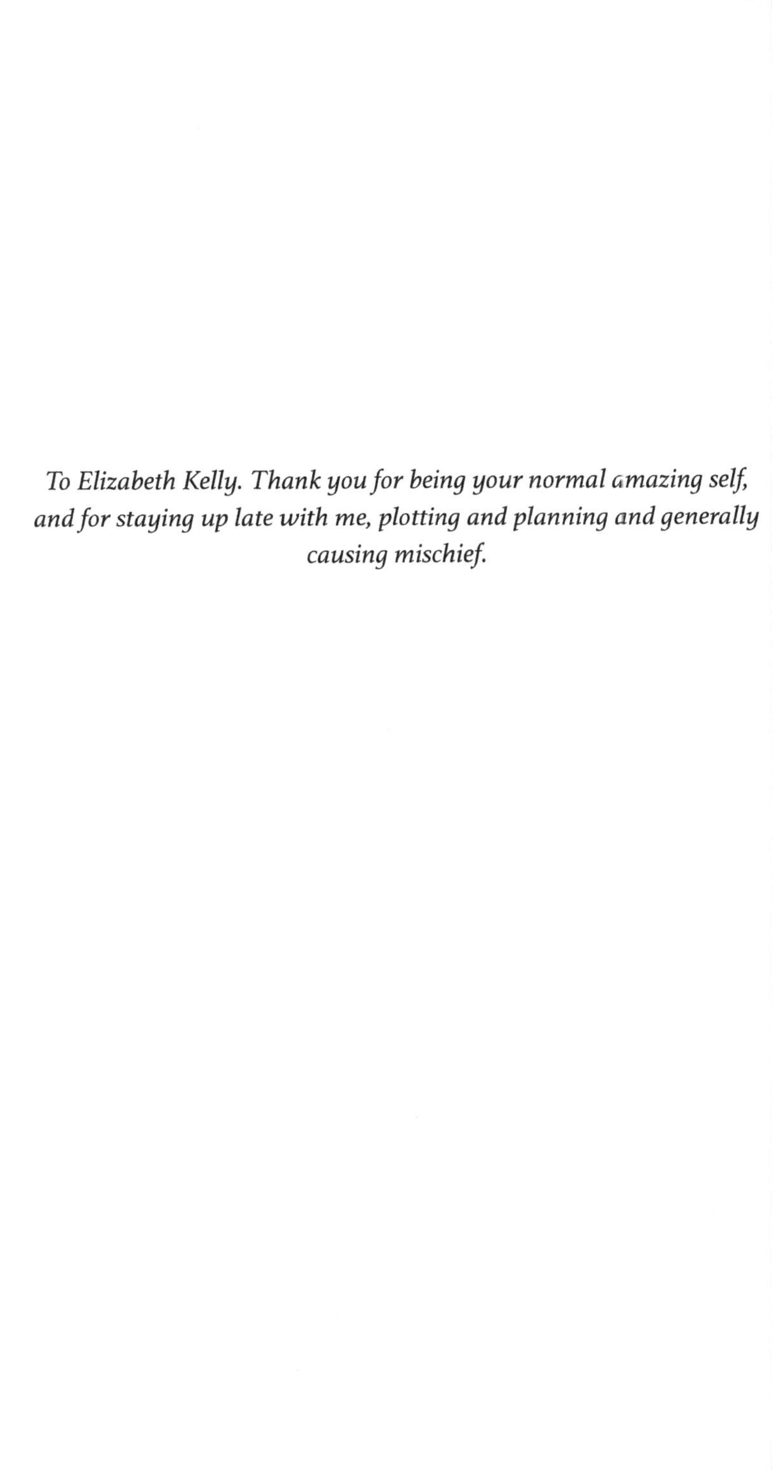

To Elizabeth Kelly. Thank you for being your normal amazing self, and for staying up late with me, plotting and planning and generally causing mischief.

LUCK OF THE DRAW

1

THE STANDS AT THE PECOS RODEO GROUNDS BUZZED WITH shouting and laughing and hollering and anticipation like the Roman Coliseum but with less blood and guts. The West Texas heat soaked Josephine Cox's shorts with sweat, and the high humidity made her wish she had gills.

She tugged on Comet's lead rope and the palomino quarter horse picked up his head from the plot of patchy grass and followed with the reluctance of a five-year-old on the way to the dentist.

You'd think Comet was slow. You'd think Comet wasn't competitive.

You'd be wrong.

At the shade covered wash rack near the warm-up arena, Josephine cross-tied Comet, and pulled the whitening shampoo out of the bucket. She wet her horse's white mane and liberally worked the shampoo into the manure-stained hair. She should have known better than to take the fly sheet off her horse that close to the start of the rodeo. Note to self: next horse would be horse-poop brown.

"There you are. I've been looking all over for you." The male voice came from somewhere on the other side of Comet. Josephine wasn't tall enough to see over her horse's withers, but she didn't have to peek under Comet's muscular neck to know who was coming.

"Looks like you found me." Forget the poop brown horse. For the first time in her life, Josephine wished she'd bought a plain-Jane sorrel. Just an all red horse, no star on his forehead, no white stocking running up its legs, just a horse like any other. A horse that was impossible to pick out in a crowd. Not one in a million that shone like a beacon and turned every head within an eight-mile radius.

Tall, and lankier than most of the other bull riders, Monte Shaw easily folded his arms over Comet's back and leaned against the stout horse. He propped his straw cowboy hat higher on his forehead, revealing brilliant blue eyes and a freshly shaved face a girl would be tempted to take home to momma if she didn't know any better.

"Come to town with me after the rodeo tonight. There's this new guy, David Allen somebody, playing at the honky tonk. Supposed to be pretty good."

"I don't know." Josephine massaged the shampoo into the base of the mane. Comet's lips twitched, and his head bobbed, and the horse let out a soft grunt. If her dream of being a pro barrel racer didn't pan out, maybe she could work the circuit as an equine masseuse.

Or heck, she'd subject herself to the makeup and the hairspray and the rhinestone-studded outfits and carry the flag if she had to. Anything would be better than landing back at the Rockin' C and settling down for the rest of her life.

"Oh, come on." He came around her horse's rump with one of those cocky half-smiles that had charmed the pants off the buckle bunnies, the barrel racers, and the riders from the flag team.

"I was going to pack up and get an early start tomorrow. Calgary is a long way away."

"And we'll have most of the week to get there. A few hours here or there won't make no difference."

She rinsed the suds from Comet's mane. Monte stepped closer. And closer. She gripped the sprayer like a weapon. At least they weren't alone. Spectators wondered by, their little kids riding stick ponies or stuffing their faces with cotton candy. Nearby, in the outdoor arena, cowboys and cowgirls warmed up their horses under the baking sun, the thick cloud of dust that the horses kicked up made the back of her throat itch. While Monte up close made her skin crawl.

He stepped forward. She stepped back. He stopped. "Come on now. Only a few weeks left until the circuit ends in Cheyenne. I was hoping to get a chance to know you better."

"It's not like you won't ever see me again. If you ride the ridge trail, your father's place is only a hard thirty-minute ride from the Rockin' C."

"That's different. Your parents are there. My parents are there. And the bad blood..."

"Maybe you should have thought of asking me out months ago, before you banged every babe south of the Mason-Dixon line."

He didn't even have the decency to look embarrassed. Instead, he took a step back and looked Josephine up and down, from the water dampened tips of her cowboy boots, to her cutoff jeans, up to last year's *Cheyenne Rodeo* T-shirt she'd knotted at her waist. His eyes lingered over the lettering covering her breasts before he met her eyes with bold confidence. "I never took you for a prude, Cox."

"I'm no prude, Monte. This is the seventies after all. You know, bras have been burned, sex has been revolutionized and all that." She waved a hand in the general direction of his crotch. "Just no telling where that thing's been."

He backed her against a nearby stall, her fingers tight on the sprayer's trigger. "What do you know about who I've slept with?" He leaned in close and whispered in her ear. "I never kiss and tell."

"Maybe not." She shoved a hand against his chest and brushed past him. She didn't have time for this. She had to get changed, and get Comet saddled and warmed up before her run. "But the girls gossip. A lot."

He grabbed her arm and spun her around. "Come on, Josie. One beer."

She dug her heels in. He tugged harder, her boots slipped in the water and she slammed against his chest. The sprayer went off in her hand. The freezing cold well water soaked them, and she let out a shriek of surprise. Monte stripped the hose from her hand and threw it down, but didn't let her go.

"L-Leave h-h-her alone."

Monte turned, her arm still tight in his grip. Rowdy Boyd stood behind them, already in his rodeo clown costume, but he hadn't put his makeup on yet. Probably didn't want it melting off under the blazing Texas summer sun.

"W-w-who's gonna s-s-stop me?" Monte mocked Rowdy's stutter.

Rowdy stood taller, but he was still more than a head shorter than Monte. "M-Me."

"Bug off, Mighty Mouse. Gotta be a racehorse out there somewhere in need of a jockey."

"You mother fucker." Rowdy launched himself at Monte. Rowdy was fast and wiry and agile. Which was probably what made him such a good bullfighter.

Out of the corner of her eye, Josephine caught a flash of blue as a man stepped between Monte and Rowdy. He pushed a hand in the middle of both men's chests, his large frame blocking Rowdy from view. *Silas Foss.*

"Get out of here, Foss," Rowdy said, "This isn't your fight." Funny how Rowdy's stutter always disappeared when he was riled.

Silas ignored Rowdy and turned his attention to Monte. "I suggest you keep your hands off the lady." Monte's grip loosened enough for Josephine to pull her arm free. "And need I remind you who's going to be out there in that arena saving your dumb ass from fifteen hundred pounds of pissed off beef?"

Monte knocked Silas's palm away from his chest and looked from Silas to Rowdy to Josephine. His expression shifting from anger to blatant interest when his eyes landed on hers. "Think about tonight."

"You've got to be kidding." The man had the nerve of a snake charmer in a pit of vipers. Josephine popped the quick release clips on the cross-ties and grabbed Comet's rope.

"C-can you believe this g-guy?" Rowdy said to Silas.

Monte pointed a finger at Rowdy as he started to back away. "You'd better do your job tonight, you little piss ant. Don't leave me hangin'—"

"Get the hell out of here." Silas put a staying hand on Rowdy's shoulder.

Monte laughed, but his focus was on Rowdy. "What's the matter baby buckaroo? You need your bodyguard—"

"I don't need you fighting my f-fights, Foss." Rowdy shook off Silas's hand, his face red, but not from the heat.

Rowdy stormed off toward his trailer before Josephine got a chance to thank him for stepping in. Monte continued to walk backwards. Either he didn't want to turn his back on Silas or—

Monte duffed his hat and pointed it at her. "I'll pick you up at your trailer after the closing ceremony."

"Why's he pickin' you up?"

Josephine spun around. Chet Orin came walking up behind her. Of all the— "What are you doing here?"

Chet pulled off his hat and laid the brim against his chest with a this-wasn't-my-idea tilt to his lips. "Your father sent me."

"My fa—" Josephine grabbed her grooming bucket. "Unbelievable." She wanted to throw the bucket at Chet's head, but mostly she wanted to throw it at her father. But he was in the Texas Hill Country, a few hundred miles away. Josephine had a good arm for a girl, but her arm wasn't that good. She backed Comet out of the wash rack. "I'm a twenty-three-year-old woman. I don't need a babysitter. Why'd he bother sending you now, after all these months?"

"Maybe if you'd bothered to call—"

She nicked him with a cutting glare.

Chet held his arms out to his sides. "I just do what I'm told."

He always had.

From the day he'd been born. From the day Chet's father had abandoned him and his mother at the Rockin' C. Obedient. Loyal. Like the son The Great Caine Cox never had.

Silas stood there with his hands on his hips. Waiting. Watching. She was already sweating, but heat rushed up her neck and landed on her cheeks. Unlike with Monte, she liked the way Silas watched her.

"Let me walk you back to your stall," Chet said.

"I don't need—"

Silas spoke up. "I'll take her."

"Wait. Not you, too?" She couldn't keep the shrill pitch of disappointment out of her voice. She didn't need a keeper. She didn't need a man. She didn't need anybody.

Comet bopped her on the arm with her nose. Okay, she needed Comet. Especially if she wanted to run barrels. But that was all she needed. She backed away, tugging Comet along with her. "Just...Just both of you, go away."

ON THE DUSTY, GRITTY OUTSKIRTS OF PECOS, TEXAS, A PLACE where tumbleweeds could roll on forever, Silas walked into the Rough Rider bar. The time was late, the crowd was thick, and the beer flowed freely. On a stage no bigger than a saddle pad, David Allen Coe had to already be well into his second set of the night. Some song about hitching a ride with Hank Williams that made Silas itch to hit the road himself.

The only thing that had stopped him was that Josephine's trailer still sat in the lot at the rodeo grounds, her horse bedded down for the night, munching away on hay. She hadn't cut out for Calgary the way her friends and most of the rest of the rodeo rats had.

He worked his way to the bar, his pockets flush with his weekend winnings. He came away with a longneck bottle of Lone Star beer in each hand, optimistic he'd find her here. He scanned the half-local, half-rodeo crowd, skirted around the dance floor, receiving back slaps and congratulations along the way. But he wasn't looking for accolades, he was looking for Josephine.

Almost giving up, he leaned against a pillar, his eyes on the stage as he took a swig from his beer.

"Do you mind? You're blocking my view."

Silas turned and smiled, not even trying to play it cool. He'd never had the time for head games. He snagged an empty chair and pulled it up to the tiny table in the corner where Josephine had hidden herself. "You're a hard person to find."

Her hair was down, and the faint ring from her cowboy hat, rimmed her head. She took a sip of her drink. The ice was mostly melted as if she'd been nursing it much of the night. "That was kind of the point."

A new song started. He pushed one of the beers towards her,

and had to raise his voice over the music to make himself heard. "You want me to leave?"

She considered his question as if it were a life-changing decision. "You did bring me a beer."

"I did. I couldn't picture you drinking the hard stuff." He picked up her glass and gave it a sniff. He smiled. "Water?"

"On the rocks. This time, but don't let this face fool you. I'm not opposed to the hard stuff on occasion." Josephine switched to the beer he'd brought her and brought it up to those perfect lips. Lips, he wanted around his—

Stop. His jeans grew tighter and last year's championship belt buckle bit into his belly. He washed the salacious thoughts away with a long swallow. He had to get his head out of the gutter.

Word on the cirbuit was Josephine Cox wasn't that kind of girl.

"Water on the rocks. Hardcore. That's what I love about you."

She sputtered and spit out her beer, wiping her mouth with the back of her hand. "What did you say?"

Her face went red and she started gathering up her purse. He was about to apologize for embarrassing her when he realized her focus had shifted to a spot over his shoulder. He turned in his seat. Chet Orin and Monte Shaw strode through the front door. She bopped Silas on the arm and he turned back around.

"You coming?" Josephine was ducking down in front of him as if trying to hide.

That was a no-brainer. "Coming."

She grabbed his hand and pulled him toward the back of the building, down the smoke-choked narrow hall with the faded autographed photos of Waylon Jennings, Lefty Frizzell, and Guy Clark. They moved quickly past the lines in front of the restrooms, and past the clang and bustle of the honky-tonk's kitchen.

She shoved through the back door, the smell of old frying oil followed them out. The door hit the back wall and slammed closed behind him, locking the sounds and the smells and the songs inside.

"What's the problem?"

She dropped his hand. "Sorry about that."

"I'm not."

A breeze kicked up, carrying the stench of rotting food from the nearby dumpster. It should have been a moment that took his breath away. And it did. But not because of the smell.

Josephine had the biggest, brownest eyes that made him think of gangly fawns before they lost their spots. But Josephine was far from gangly, and during her time on the circuit she had proven that she wasn't easy prey.

Josephine stilled. "Look, Foss, I'm not looking for a fling, or a buckle to hang my belt beside every night."

Silas leaned a shoulder against the brick building, and pushed his hat higher on his head as he schooled his smile. He was kicking himself for not making a move earlier in the season. "You're the one who pulled me out here, remember?"

Something shuttered behind her eyes. "Right. My mistake."

She turned to leave, but Silas caught her arm. "Hang on. You never answered my question. What's the problem with those guys?"

"No problem."

"Riiight." He crossed his arms over his chest. Josephine was a crappy liar. "As soon as you saw Monte and Chet you bolted down that hallway like a skittish horse at an amateur rodeo."

Like him, she crossed her arms. *Don't look at her boobs, don't look at her boobs, don't look at her boobs.* He glued his eyes to hers. He was attracted, but he wasn't a dog.

"I'm just tired. The circuit seems extra-long this year, and I'm tired of playing the mouse to Monte's cat. And if that's not bad enough, my father has his best trained cattle dog nipping at my heels. They're the last two people I wanted to see tonight."

The breeze swirled, kicking dirt and leaves into a stinky dust devil. Josephine's nose wrinkled. "I should be getting back. There's a patch of grass behind the stands. I want to graze Comet before I go to bed."

They walked toward their trucks. He wanted to reach out and take her hand, to feel the sweet contrast again between her soft skin and her calloused palms. But like she'd said, she wasn't looking for a relationship.

The nomadic rodeo life was more suited to tantalizing trysts than long-lasting relationships. Not that he'd decline if she offered.

He was parked across the lot from her truck, but he walked her to her driver's side door.

"Thanks," she said. "You didn't have to walk me out."

The single light at the top of a nearby utility pole left much of the gravel lot in the dark. "Yeah. I did."

She unlocked her door and tossed her purse inside. In the glow from her dome light, he spotted the finger sized bruising on her arm. Anger heated his veins. A slow, insidious burn. "Monte do that to you?"

"I can handle Monte." Standing in the pocket behind her open truck door, she held her hand over the bruising as if it could make him unsee what he'd seen. "I handled Lloyd Cagle a few weeks back, didn't I?"

"I hear he's still spending his nights icing his bruised balls." Silas chuckled, an unanticipated warmth settling in his chest for this woman. She was unlike anyone he'd ever been with before, and he found that both refreshing and enticing. He'd had enough success on the circuit that he got his fair share of attention from the ladies. You'd think being treated like you're something special wouldn't get old.

It did.

The front door of the bar swung open and Rowdy stumbled out with a woman on each arm.

"Awh," Josephine said, "that's so sweet."

Sweet? Silas chuckled. "He's looking to get laid." The words were out of his mouth before he could filter them, and here he'd thought he was over that concussion from last month.

But instead of being offended, Josephine laughed, too. It wasn't musical. It was off-pitch and had the most adorable snort at the end. He couldn't take his eyes off her. *Josephine Cox. Where have you been all my life?*

"Yeah, but he's a nice guy. It's good to see him getting some female attention for a change."

"That news report last month didn't hurt. You would have thought he'd taken a bullet for the president."

"He did save Cooper's life. That bull was bent on breaking him and making him bleed, and Rowdy got you out of that mess with Thunderclap tonight. With your hand caught in the rigging, that tight spin the bull had you in, I thought that it would—" The way she cocked her head at him reminded him of a puzzled puppy. "Why do you have that goofy grin?"

"You watched my ride?" He'd had his eye on her for months, sometime before Houston. The fact that she'd noticed him, watched him, made him want to puff his chest out and strut around like a proud peacock. Monte Shaw could suck his—

She mumbled something he didn't catch. With a finger under her chin, he tilted her head up, glad the open truck door partially protected him from a well-placed boot tip in case she thought he was getting too fresh. "What was that?"

She didn't pull away. "I said, I had a spare moment."

The warmth in his chest spread wider. He dropped his hand, even though he wanted to brush his thumb over that bottom lip. That bottom lip that begged to be nibbled.

"Shouldn't you have been cooling off your horse instead of watching the bullriding?"

"I managed."

Behind him, the girls giggled as the threesome got closer. Those kind of giggles used to make Silas hard. Now they just made him shudder.

When Rowdy was a car length away, Josephine said, "Great job, tonight."

Silas stuck out his hand and Rowdy released one of the ladies long enough to shake hands. "Yeah, thanks, again."

"I appreciate that. But I was only doing my job." Looked like lust got rid of Rowdy's stutter, too.

The threesome scooted between a Ford Fairlane and a rattle-trap GMC pickup and disappeared into the dark. Silas stepped beside Josephine. His hand cupping her cheek before he had time for conscious thought.

"What are you doing?"

She didn't pull away, and she didn't kick him either. It was practically an open invitation, so he eased closer. "I'm going to kiss you Josephine Cox. If that's not what you want, you need to say so now."

"You can have any woman you want. Why me?"

He couldn't deny it. The more he'd won, the more the women skittered out of the woodwork like he was a tasty morsel of bull riding meat.

But she was Caine Cox's daughter. In Texas, beef was big, and Cox was king. Which made Silas a peasant to Josephine's princess. But Josephine was also different than the other women on and around the circuit in a way he'd been unable to ignore these last few months. He didn't have an answer for her question. Instead he said, "Is that a yes or a no?"

She leaned in as her tongue wet her bottom lip. A yes then.

His hand went around the back of her neck, his fingers tangling in her soft, lazy curls. He bent his head and—

A hand clapped him on the back. "Hands off the merchandise, Foss." *Chet Orin.* Silas swallowed the growl.

Josephine jumped and squeaked, but Silas hardly had time to get angry at Chet before she brushed past him and got in Chet's face, or rather, his chest. She was so close she had to tilt her head back to look the guy in the eye. "Go away." With a finger, she prodded him in the sternum. "Far, far, away."

Silas pushed his hat back and crossed his arms. "I'd do what the lady says if I were you."

Chet spared Silas a quick glare then pinned the look on Josephine. "If your father—"

The slap came fast and sharp. Chet's head snapped to the side and he took a step back.

"Shoulda listened." Silas liberally coated his words with I-told-you-so's.

Josephine pointed toward the back of the lot, her lithe body tensed and ready for a fight. The last time Silas had seen her that mad, future generations of Cagles had been obliterated. "*Go.*"

Was it wrong that her fire lubed Silas's gears?

Chet backed a couple steps before turning and walking away. The fact that Chet rubbed at his jaw as he left gave Silas more satisfaction than going the full eight seconds in the short go.

Josephine climbed into her truck and slammed the door. She didn't drive away. She gripped the wheel and yanked and yanked as if she wanted to tear the steering wheel from the column. Then she yelled. Even with her window closed, her frustration hit Silas like a bull stomp to the chest. Then she dropped her hands and sat there in her seat, staring out the windshield, her chest rising and falling in large gasps that fogged the windows.

He gave her a moment. Two. Did she even remember he was

there? He rapped his knuckle on the window. Nothing. He rapped again. She reached over and cranked the window down, the glass making a *scree-scree-scree* sound as it scraped against something inside the door frame.

"You okay?" He asked.

"Sure." Her pitch was off, but that wasn't unexpected.

"Wait here while I grab my truck. I'll follow you back to the rodeo grounds."

"I don't need—"

"*Josephine.*"

"*What?*"

He smiled when she mimicked the exasperation in his tone. "Humor me."

She huffed out a breath and her breathing returned to normal. She didn't answer, but she nodded. He took a step to leave when she said, "Oh, Fossy?"

He turned back, his hands on the sill of her door as the warmth blooming in his chest made something ignite. "Fossy? No one's called me that since grade school." He hadn't like it then, but coming from her mouth, from those lips...it taunted him. In a good way. "What do you need?"

"Thank you."

"For what? I didn't do anything. You had the situation under control."

"Exactly." She smiled at him. It was big and bedazzling.

It was bold and bodacious.

It was trouble.

No. *She* was trouble.

2

———

Friday night found Josephine sitting on an upturned bucket inside Comet's stall at the rodeo grounds in Calgary. The best thing she could say about Calgary was that it wasn't Pecos. Oh, and being so far north, at least it cooled off at night and she wouldn't parboil in her trailer while she slept.

Her horse was tied, munching hay as his right rear hoof soaked in a shallow feed bowl filled with an Epsom salt and Betadine mixture. She glanced at her watch. Five more minutes. She dropped her head back against the wall. As her eyes drifted closed, she wished for the end of her sucky, sucky day.

Comet chuffed a welcome around a mouthful of hay, and Josephine startled awake.

Silas leaned a muscular shoulder against the open stall door. He was still dressed in his looser pair of jeans the bull riders used for competition, but had changed into a western shirt that probably hadn't seen starch since well before Pecos. "I hear Terry Lewis has an open bunk in his trailer if you need a place to sleep."

"Terry, don't-call-me-Jerry, Lewis? The stockman?"

"The one and only."

She wrinkled her nose. "Thanks, but Comet's stall has fewer flies buzzing around it than Lewis's trailer. Besides, I'm just about done here, and I have my tack compartment to myself tonight."

"You don't say." Silas's tone came out equal parts open curiosity and...was that...naked invitation?

Josephine shook herself awake, certain she'd only heard what she'd wanted to hear. Silas didn't have Monte's classic ranch-boy-next-door good looks, or the massive arms of the bulldoggers. He was a fine, rugged man and there was something about his confidence, his sincerity, his integrity, his heart, that pushed all her go-go buttons.

They had been running into each other more in the two weeks on either side of the Pecos rodeo than they ever had in all the time since Houston in the early spring. Coincidence?

Nope. She didn't believe in coincidences.

His hat shaded his eyes from the glare of the overhead lights, but something in the way he stood there, drew her attention. Whether it was the turn of his head, the easy way he leaned there, feigning a calm, cool, and content cowboy, when the tension in his shoulders said he was anything but that.

He tucked his thumbs into the front pockets of his jeans, and his long fingers fell over the front of his Wranglers. She tried not to stare, but the term "hung like a bull" came to mind. She really had to stop spending so much time with Cora. She was a bad, bad, influence.

Silas bobbed his head toward Comet's rear hoof. "What happened?"

Her stomach slid to a stop faster than Jester's roping horse. When the acid settled, she said, "Threw a shoe coming around the third barrel. Got a puncture in the sole from one of the nails. Must have come down on it before he lost it completely. I'm trying to keep him from abscessing."

Silas made one of those *that sucks* faces. "Oh, man. Bad luck."

She didn't believe in luck, any more than she believed in coincidences. When things happened, they happened for a reason. *If Comet abscesses, what's the reason for that? Does that mean you have no business riding the circuit?*

Does that mean father was right?

No. She refused to believe it meant that. *What*, it meant she didn't know. But not *that*.

Silas cleared his throat. "Mind if I join you?"

"I was just leaving," she said, though she was too worn out to bother getting up.

He slipped behind her horse, knocked an errant ball of manure out of the way, and started easing himself onto the clean pile of shavings next to her. Partway down, he caught himself with a hand on her shoulder, hissed in a breath, and clapped an arm over his ribs. He grunted as he sat.

"What the heck, Fossy?"

"I'm fine."

"You're not fine. Let me see." She dropped to her knees in front of him and tugged the tail of his shirt out of his jeans. "Holy mackerel."

"Shouldn't that be holy cow? Or maybe holy bull?"

"You're not funny. Don't give up your day job." A raised purple bruise covered his ribs. "On second thought, maybe you should give up your day job."

Her hand went to his side, and he hissed in a breath.

"That hurt?"

"No. Sweet Jesus, your hands are cold!" He gathered her hands in his and started rubbing the heat back into them. Only his touch heated way more than her hands, making her wonder for the first time, if her promise to forgo men while riding the circuit would be that big of a deal to break.

Wait. Yeah. It was a big deal.

Affairs led to engagements, which led to marriages, and then the next thing you knew, a promising future chasing cans had turned into a lifetime of chasing kids.

Not that there was anything wrong with that.

But she had goals. She had dreams. Goals and dreams that didn't involve her staying home and waiting week after week for a break in the circuit schedule, or for the rodeo to swing close enough for her to see her man again.

She pulled her hands away from his and went to stand up.

He grabbed her wrist. "Did I do something wrong?"

"No." The word came out too fast and too high pitched to be believable.

"Then what's with that someone-stole-my-horse face?"

"That's my what-the-heck-are-you-doing-here-when-you-need-ice face." She slapped her hands to her cheeks, dropped her jaw and made her eyes go wide. "This is my someone-stole-my-horse face."

He laughed, but it was cut short by string of curses. He curled in on himself. "Damn. Don't make me laugh."

She sat back on her heels. "Sorry. But really, what happened? I thought that bull you drew was supposed to be nice."

"You checked my draw?" One corner of his mouth tipped up and he got a spark in his eye. The Silas equivalent of a wide grin.

"That's beside the point. Answer the question."

He sat his hat beside him and leaned his head against the wall. Despite the chill in the air, his short brown hair was sweaty around his head where his hatband had rested. "The bull was nice. *Too* nice. He came out of the chute, spun once to the left, once to the right then took me on a victory lap around the arena."

"So you got a reride?"

"Yeah. Wasn't so lucky that time. Some bull by the name of The Man Eater or The Maimer or—"

"You mean Bone Crusher?"

He pointed a finger at her and gave her a wink which she refused to admit did stupid, silly things to her stomach. "That's him. Determined to live up to his name. He tossed me after the buzzer, then danced on my ribs to congratulate me."

"Ouch."

He grinned—part humor, part grimace, part pain—and held out his hand. "Help me up."

She didn't take his hand. "You stay put. I'm going to get Comet settled, then we'll put ice on those ribs."

Silas settled back, covering his face with his hat. Josephine hurried through her chores—hoof dried off, hay net stuffed, water buckets filled. Check, check and check. She freed Comet in the stall and tapped Silas on the bottom of his boot. "Rise and shine, cowboy."

Silas rested an arm on his knee, and glanced up at her. "What's wrong?"

"Nothing."

"Nothing, hell." He pointed at her face. "You've got the Grand Canyon carved between your brows."

She reached up and smoothed out the furrow. "I think this circuit is cursed. Or there's bad juju. Something."

He laughed, then groaned with pain. When she didn't laugh with him he sobered. "You're serious."

Comet put his chin on her shoulder and snuffled in her ear. She scratched his nose. "First that bull rider, Cooper, almost gets killed last month, and a few others are hurt. Tonight, you got stomped."

Silas raised his hands. "That's not bad juju. That's bull riding."

"There's been other things. Cora said one of the ropers'

horses bowed a tendon, and then Comet lost a brand new shoe and..."

"And what?"

"And as much as I don't want this circuit to end. It will almost be a relief when we all finish in Cheyenne, hopefully in one piece."

"All that, that's the nature of the beast. Bad things happen."

She made one of those I-don't-think-so faces, but she was too tired to argue. She held out a hand for him.

He groaned and locked his hand around her wrist. Helping him get up took a lot of grunting on her part and a lot of cussing on his. "Still think you don't need the ice?"

It wasn't meant to be rhetorical, but he didn't answer like it was.

She'd just gotten him steady on his feet when several large banks of overhead lights blinked out. "I guess that's our cue to leave."

There were still some lights on at the end of the aisles. Enough at least for them to stumble their way out of the stall. She pulled a pocket-fuzzed carrot from her jeans, brushed it off, and gave it to Comet, scratching the fine bristles on the end of his soft nose while he chewed. She turned to leave and bumped into Silas.

"*Ooof.*" He caught her by the shoulders and steadied himself.

He backed her against the stall door. Comet shuffled over and nibbled and tugged on her ponytail, but as Silas stepped one muscular thigh between her own, she stopped noticing what her horse was doing.

Silas's hands slid up her arms and across her shoulders until his thumbs brushed the pounding pulse at the base of her neck. He ducked his head. She knew what was coming and met him halfway.

Their lips touched, a tantalizing slide of skin on skin. She smelled the hops on his breath, the roughstock on his skin, and something else that made her think of clear nights and the rugged hill country...home.

He came back in for a second run. She wanted to cup the back of his neck, to pull him closer, to deepen the kiss. But he pulled away, resting his forehead on hers. His breath hitched and she didn't know if it was his ribs or her that had affected him. He shifted and his erection brushed against her belly.

Her then. She smiled.

"That was a beautiful run you and Comet had tonight."

What? Her brain slipped a gear then caught. "Uh, thanks?" There was a time for compliments and a time to shut up. This was one of those times he needed to shut up and kiss her.

Without saying anything else, he stepped closer and pressed up against her. She could hear him breathing. No. Wait. That was her. She reached up to grab his shirt, but stopped. Why had he stopped kissing her? Was something wrong?

Did she have bad breath?

Had her kiss been as desperate as she'd felt?

Did it show that she hadn't been laid since the start of the indoor season last fall?

She opened to mouth to ask, but her questions didn't tumble out. Instead she said, "It wasn't our fastest time considering the thrown shoe, and Comet knocked the second barrel and we're near the bottom of the standings and Dottye Goodspeed doesn't run until tomorrow so she could knock us out of the finals and there's a good reason *speed* is in her last name and—"

"Whoa, whoa, whoa. Relaaax." He pressed another kiss to her forehead, to the corner of her eye. He kissed his way down her jawline until he'd made it back to her lips. He was no longer exploring, but tasting. He opened her mouth with his and dove in.

Kissing was better than talking anyway.

Their tongues taunted and tangled.

His hands slid to the curve of her ass, and snaked up under the hem of her untucked shirt, his calloused hands hot against her skin. He broke the kiss long enough for both of them to suck in a couple of quick breaths, then went back for more. She slid her arms around his neck as he lifted her up and wrapped her legs around—

"Aaaghhhh." He stumbled and dropped her.

She grabbed onto the rail of the stall front to keep from falling. "Ohmygod, ohmygod. I'm sorry. Are you okay?"

He was bent over, his right hand braced on his knee, his left arm hugging his ribs. His breaths coming shallow and quick.

"Silas?"

He held a finger up in a way that said give-me-a-second.

"I'm so, so sorry. I don't know what I was thinking."

When he caught his breath, he straightened, as slow as a ninety-two-year-old man. But even in the darkened barn, she saw what might have qualified as a smile on his face.

"What are you smiling about?" she asked.

"The fact that I could make you not think." He reached out for her but she lightly batted his hand away.

"Uh, uh, cowboy. No more kissing until you ice those ribs."

His teeth flashed in the light with a grin she'd expect to see on one of the painted up rodeo clowns.

"What?"

"That implies there's going to be a next time."

She figured an emphatic *oh hell yeah*, probably made her sound desperate, so she kept it to herself.

Silas walked her to her trailer. The door to her front tack compartment, aka home-sweet-home, stood wide open.

"I swear I don't know what to do with Cora." Josephine yanked a flashlight out of the tray in the door and shined the light around inside. "Ever since she's been hanging out with that roper, her head's been so high in the clouds, I think the extra moisture has rusted her synapses."

"Everything still there?"

Her and Cora's saddles were locked in the back of the trailer so at least the most important things were safe. "Looks like."

She went to click off the light, but Silas took it from her hands and leaned in, having a look around. "Cozy. You're not afraid Cora's bunk is going to fall on you in the middle of the night?"

"Adrenaline junkies like living on the edge."

"Touché"

Silas swung the light over the rest of the space. From the stacked double bunks, to the short rod for their hanging clothes that Chet had helped install before she'd set out in the spring, to the set of six stacking milk crates she and Cora used to store the rest of their things, to her extra pair of boots in the corner, complete with caked on mud that she hadn't found the time to clean.

In the back of the trailer she had rigged a makeshift shower and a small porta-potty. Which made her rig luxurious compared to some of the other competitors. But she was confident Silas didn't want or need to see that too.

That was it. There wasn't even enough square footage to call it the ten cent tour. More like the tarnished and dented half-penny tour.

"It doesn't get a little tight in there?" This from a man with a cab-over camper on his truck. In comparison, it looked like she and Cora were living in a soup can. Which they pretty much were.

"Cora's tight on funds and she's my best friend. We make it work." Josephine wasn't exactly flush either. Especially after not pulling a check at the last two rodeos. But she had a good feeling about the finals on Sunday if Comet stayed sound and her time held.

He brushed the hair off one of her shoulders, his breath warm on her neck as he leaned in and whispered. "I guess bringing a guy back to your place is out of the question."

The deep rumble of his voice sent a shiver down her spine and all the hair stood up on her arms and waved *hello!* She wouldn't admit the truth. That the lack of privacy hadn't been a problem because she'd been too focused on her career for it to matter. "We make it work."

But for the first time in months she wondered what was the harm in a little distraction.

Her father would tell her to take up knitting.

Her grandmother—bless her dirty old heart—would tell her to take up men.

Josephine went to close her trailer door. It was late, and they still had Silas's ribs to ice. He caught the door and said, "Good night, Josie."

What? "I was going to help you ice those ribs."

He waited a beat. It dragged on and on like those times when she'd waited at the pay phones while the line rang and rang as she tried to make the entry cutoff for the next rodeo. Only usually her stomach didn't feel like the air was leaking out. Had she misread him? Was he trying to find a nice way to let her down?

"You've had a long day. Get some sleep. I can take care of the ribs."

Her stomach did that *pfffffft* thing that balloons do when someone lets go of the end and all the air escapes and the rubber zips and dips and crashes. She tried to clear her throat of her doubts, but they stuck in her windpipe. "Y-yeah. Sure. I could use a few Zs."

They exchanged *good nights* and Silas walked away.

No hesitation.

No looking back.

Josephine climbed into her trailer and closed the door behind her. The front of her trailer had about a foot-long horizontal window that matched the curve of the nose. Standing on top of one of the milk crates, she could just make out the back of Silas's rig sticking out from behind a stock trailer. Then the tail lights of the stock trailer came on and someone towed it out of her line of sight.

A light was visible in Silas's camper. But even with the shades drawn she knew he wasn't icing his ribs because his cooler laid upturned beside his truck, the lid open as if he were letting it dry out.

She flopped on her bunk. It shifted. Metal groaned. Her breath caught. The bunk held. She closed her eyes, but her insides jigged and jogged in place the same way Comet did in the alley before a run. With all her worrying, she wasn't going to get any sleep, she was going to get a migraine.

She climbed out of the trailer, grabbed Comet's spare water bucket, and went in search of ice.

She didn't know if Silas hadn't wanted to ice his ribs or if he hadn't wanted her.

But there was only one way to find out.

3

SILAS SAT ON THE BENCH SEAT OF HIS DINETTE, A COUPLE PILLOWS
from the bed propped up behind him as he read a Louis
L'Amour book that had been making the rounds. He went to
turn the page, but it stuck to the one behind it. The book was
tattered and the way some of the pages were wrinkled and wavy,
it might have gone two rounds with a water trough.

He pried the pages free, but some of the letters came off and
stuck to the other page making it impossible to read. He dog-
eared a corner and set the book on the table. The light overhead
dimmed as his battery weakened.

Without the book to distract him, he started thinking of
Josephine and everything he wanted to do with those lips and
those hips and—

Tap, tap, tap. The knock was light, hesitant.

It wasn't his best friend, Tobias. That man used the meat of
his fist and pounding like the big bad wolf.

He stared at the door and debated pretending he was asleep.
But it was late and no one knocked on doors this deep into the
night unless someone's horse got out, or someone was in
trouble.

Knock, knock, knock. Louder now. More insistent. It would be hard to pretend to sleep through that.

He grabbed the end of the table and hauled himself up. The quick movement sent shooting pains across his ribs and he hissed in a breath. "Yeah, yeah. Keep your pants on."

He shoved the door open. "Josephine...what are you doing here?" *So the bucket of ice in her hand wasn't a big enough clue?* He sounded like his brain was packed with more sawdust than the championship stall at the Quarter Horse Congress.

Josephine raised the bucket and shook it. "Can I come in?"

He wanted to drag her into his camper, strip all their clothes off, and lock themselves away from the world until Cheyenne. Or longer. Probably not what she thought she was getting herself into tonight. "Uhhh..."

Her face fell the same way it always did when she and Comet have had a bad run.

She set the bucket at his feet on the floor of the camper. "Or not. I'm sure you're plenty capable. I just noticed your cooler was empty and figured you didn't have any ice and so I found Cora and they had bought some and—"

"No, no. Come in." He loved the way her nose crinkled, and all her sentences ran together when she got flustered.

He pushed the door all the way open, and bent to pick up the bucket, but that wasn't going to happen without serious pain meds, and he was saving what he had left for a time when he really needed them. Like before he rode in the finals on Sunday.

"Go on. I got it." She came up the steps, the leaf springs on his old truck creaking under her weight.

He backed to the dinette and use the table to ease himself onto the seat. He didn't want her seeing how much effort it took to slide in, so he let his legs dangle in the walkway.

"You want to do it here or on the bed?"

His head snapped up and he caught her eye. Her cheeks turned the color of his favorite red bandanna.

She waved a hand at him. "That came out wrong. Do you want me to—"

"I know what you meant. Here's fine."

"This would be easier if you were laying down. Does the dinette turn into a bed?"

"Yeah you just—" He started to get up, but she put a staying hand on his bare shoulder.

"You just sit there and look pretty. I've got this."

Look pretty. Damn she was something. And he was a little ashamed that that simple touch was all it took to get him hard. Good thing his sweat pants were loose. Maybe there was enough ice in the bucket to dump on his crotch as well.

In a matter of minutes, she'd folded the legs of the table, and repositioned the cushions, and turned his dinette into another bed. He wanted to reach for her, to drag her beneath him, to—

"*Fossy?*"

"Yeah?"

She fluffed the pillows and put them in the corner, so he could lean back. "Is this going to be comfortable enough for you?"

"Yeah, fine." He held a protective hand over his ribs and slid over, trying not to sound like a crippled old bull needing to be put out to pasture, or worse, put out of its misery.

When he got situated, he glanced up at her. She sat on the edge of the table-turned-bed, with one of those stern looks on her face his mother used to get when he'd let the dogs in the pig pen. He pushed the thought from his mind. The last thing he wanted to think about when he had a beautiful woman in his bed, was his mother.

"You positive nothing is broken?"

He opened his mouth, but before the *I'm fine* could escape, she held a finger to his lips and narrowed her eyes. "Think twice before you lie to me."

He held back the smile that wanted to take over his face. It would probably be hard to convince her he wasn't laughing *at* her, and the way his side was feeling, even as small as she was, she could take him.

"Doesn't feel like it."

"What do you mean 'It doesn't feel like it?'" She pitched her voice higher, mimicking him.

He hadn't sounded anything like that. At least he hoped he hadn't. That would be embarrassing.

"Wait. You didn't get checked out?"

"X-rays cost money."

"I'm pretty sure it's a solid investment. What if your ribs are broken? What if you come off again on Sunday—"

He held his hand up to get a word in but she batted it away and kept on going. "Because I know you're just stubborn enough to ride on Sunday even though any doctor with any sense would tell you you'd be a complete and total idiot to ride."

"Good thing you're not a doctor. Your bedside manners are terrible."

"You're impossible." She stood, opening, and slamming cabinet doors.

He would have asked her what she was looking for, but he was a smart man and kept his trap shut. She found a hand towel in one of the upper cabinets and wrapped it around a couple of handfuls of ice and pressed it to his ribs. He propped a hand behind his head. She wouldn't look him in the eye, her jaw hard set.

He put his hand over hers. "Look at me." She did. The anger in her eyes stung like a lick from a stock whip. "I know what cracked ribs feel like. I'm bruised, not broken."

Her expression softened enough for her exhaustion to show in the ever-dimming light above the dinette.

"Go back to your trailer and get some sleep. I've got this."

"Nope." Her voice wasn't hard, but it was quick and sure, and he'd already pissed her off enough that he decided not to fight. She pulled a small container out of her pocket. "I'm not leaving until you're iced, and I've put this ointment on your bruise. I used it on Comet when Cora's gelding kicked him in the chest with both barrels. It's effective. Just ask Comet."

Hard to argue with a horse. He let go of the ice and took the container from her hand and set it on the cushion beside him. He caught the towel back up. He had goosebumps on his chest and water had started leaking down his side into the waistband of his sweats. Her eyes drifted closed, then she caught herself.

"It's after one in the morning," he said. "I can put it on later. Go. I'm good."

She shook her head. "The same way you put ice on your ribs like you said you would?"

He pulled one of the pillows from behind his head and tossed it to her. "Lay down. At least until the time's up on the ice."

She relented, which went to show how tired she was. She hugged the pillow to her, and curled up around it, her eyes drifting closed as soon as she'd settled.

When the time was up, he dropped the towel and the melted ice back in the bucket on the counter behind his head. He waited five minutes, ten, and watched her sleep.

The fixture overhead had dimmed to the intensity of a night light, but it was enough to see her and the way her lashes brushed her cheek. He wanted to brush the hair away from her face, but he didn't want to wake her.

As much as he liked the idea of her rubbing the ointment on his skin, he'd rather she rested. He reached for the container, but she'd moved it farther down the bed when she'd laid down. He'd have to do a sideways crunch to reach it.

He could do this, he could do this, he could do this.

He gritted his teeth, wished he had a leather strap trapped between his incisors. That would help. At least it always had in all those L'Amour novels.

Okay. One. Two. Three...four. Okay. Okay. He crunch-lunged for the ointment. "*Fuuuuuck.*"

Make that eighty percent sure no bones were broken.

Josephine popped up, and she brushed the tumble of hair from her face and the trace of slobber from her lips. She grabbed the container from his hand. "Why didn't you wake me?"

Pain made the sweat break out over his forehead and he sunk back into the pillows. "Sorry, I didn't want to wake you."

"You were supposed to wake me. In fact, I wasn't supposed to be asleep."

"You were tired."

"That's no excuse." She unscrewed the lid and dipped her fingers in. "You got a flashlight? I can hardly see you."

He bumped his chin toward the counter behind him. There's a small one in the top drawer."

She got up on her knees, and had leaned over to reach the drawer. Her shirt drew up and from his vantage point, he caught a flash of her naked breast beneath her sweatshirt. He put his hand behind his head again to keep from reaching out, from cupping it, from tugging it to his mouth.

With his other hand, he reached down and loosened the string on his sweatpants and tried to think of other things, like if Caine Cox would black both his eyes or just shoot him, if the man knew what Silas wanted to do to his little girl.

That helped. A little.

Josephine settled beside him, her legs crossed, her lips around the flashlight like—

"Give me that."

"What?" With her mouth full, it sounded more like *whuuut.*

He plucked the light out of her mouth. It hurt him in more ways than one to take that flashlight from her lips, but he had a serious issue brewing behind a thin piece of cotton that he'd be better off keeping to himself.

He shined the light on his ribs and she started rubbing at the center of the bruising, slowly, working her way outward in ever increasing circles. It hurt, but the pain was bearable, especially if it meant she had her warm hands on him.

She continued rubbing his skin long after the ointment had soaked in. His skin buzzed and tingled under her fingertips. Some of it was the medication.

Most of it wasn't.

Then her hand drifted over, bumping across the muscles in his lower abdomen, beneath his belly button, her pinky finger dipping beneath the edge of his sweatpants. Holy sweet mother of—

He dropped the light and grabbed her wrist.

———

SILAS'S HAND ENGULFED HER WRIST AND HELD IT STEADY. HEAT rose to her cheeks but that didn't stop Josephine from wanting a touch, a peek, a taste of what he had beneath the tenting of his sweats. "Sorry, that was...I mean... I uh..."

She tried to back off the bed, but his grip was firm.

"Where you going?"

She preferred wallowing in her humiliation without an audience. "Back to my trailer."

The flashlight had caught at an odd angle on one of the

pillows. It shot harsh light up at Silas's face, reminding her of a kid telling ghost stories around a campfire, but even then, she saw the softness in his eyes.

He settled lower on the bed. "Kiss me." The words didn't come out as a demand or a command. They came out as a promise. A promise of what, Josephine didn't know. He gave her wrist a gentle tug, and his lips tilted up at the corners. "Kiss me."

You heard the man.

It was a tad disconcerting she'd hear those words in her naughty granny's voice. Yet despite granny's naughtiness, she had always been a smart woman.

Silas released Josephine's wrist and she crawled back to him. He gathered her hair over one shoulder, his fingers working the tight muscles at the base of her skull as she leaned in and brushed his upper lip with the tip of her tongue.

A groan of pleasure. A grunt of pain. He raised up on one elbow, opening his mouth to her, deepening the kiss. He drew back a moment, his eyes locking on hers before he dove back in for more. His arm came around the small of her back, drawing her in. Not wanting to crush his ribs with her weight, she leaned on one elbow and balanced with one leg between his.

He hitched his hand behind her thigh, shifting her on top of him. His erection pressed against her lower belly, and his hand slid beneath her jeans and cupped her curves.

A heaviness settled between her legs, as she pressed against him. As much as she wanted to reach down and take hold of the hard length of him, she broke the kiss instead. "What are we doing?"

He removed his hand from her waistband and skimmed it up her side, leaving a trail of goosebumps in its wake. "Pretty sure it's called foreplay. You know those things you do to turn your partner on and—"

"Yeah, I know what foreplay is. What's the end game here?"

As their breathing returned to normal, his expression shifted. She expected anger or frustration, but all she saw was patience and humor. "Sex? Not that you always have to end up there, but if you don't ride the bull for the full eight seconds every once in a while, you miss out on a lot of fun."

"I'm sorry." She sat up, turning her back to him and dangling her feet over the side of the bed. "I didn't mean it to come out that way. It's not like I'm looking for a proposal, or a boyfriend or..." she shut up before she embarrassed herself even more.

He huffed and puffed and grunted and groaned until he'd made it to the edge of the bed, his shoulder brushing hers. She couldn't look him in the eye. All she wanted to do was to hit a giant *redo* button and start the whole damn day over. Then she'd stay in her trailer like a good girl.

He reached over and linked their fingers. "I don't know what the end game is either. What I do know, is that I'm interested, and not in a one-and-done kind of way. By the way you had your tongue down my throat, I'm thinking that makes you interested too."

"Cheyenne is only a few weeks away and then we go our separate ways. Long distance relationships never work and—"

"Whoa now." He pressed a lingering kiss to the back of her hand and that touch settled her more than the words had. "Let's not get ahead of ourselves. I mean, who knows, I may find out that you fart like a bronc or snore as loud as a freight liner." He glanced away then looked back up at her, his eyes earnest when he said, "Please tell me you don't snore as loud as a freight liner."

"I don't snore."

"See, then there's hope for us, yet."

She got that itch between her shoulder blades that made her skin prick and her legs want to run. She wasn't looking for a happily ever after. She stood up and swayed with an exhaustion that had settled deep into her bones. His hand held her steady, but she needed to make her intentions clear so there would be no misunderstandings or hurt feelings. "I'm not looking for an us."

He tugged her back down to the bed and she didn't have the energy to resist.

"Then let's take it one day, one night at a time. Deal?"

She nodded once as her eyes drifted closed. She could do that.

"Lay down, Josie."

"What?"

"You're falling asleep sitting up. Lay down." He eased down against the wall, and fluffed the other pillow for her. He held out his hand. "Come here."

She laid next to him, her back to his chest. She shifted, and bumped up against the hard length of him, but instead of pulling her tighter against him, he angled away.

"Ignore that." His words came out tight and tense and for a brief second, she wondered what it would take to break his control.

But that wasn't what they'd agreed to.

His hand settled around her hip. "Get some sleep."

Except she didn't.

Couldn't.

Hour after hour, she lay there. His warm breath on her neck, his large hand spanning her belly, her bottom in his lap. He slept, soundless and deep, but her body buzzed with an awareness she couldn't shut off or unplug. The Naugahyde cushions squeaked when she shifted, and Silas's scent drifted up from the pillow she'd borrowed. A heady combination of sunshine and fresh air and raw power.

When the morning pinked the windows of the trailer, she didn't wait for him to wake up, because that's what couples did. They woke up together.

She slipped from beneath his arm, slid on her boots and climbed out of the trailer, her mood off and her eyes gritty from lack of sleep. She already dreaded the chores ahead of her and was counting the minutes until she could fall back in her bed. Alone.

She hadn't been looking to become a couple. She'd been looking for some fun.

$$4$$

The cool heat of a Canadian Saturday afternoon found Josephine three hoof soaks and two short naps later. She snapped on her farrier chaps and worked her fingers into the sweat hardened leather of a pair of old work gloves complete with rasp-warn fingers.

People had been giving her a wide berth all day, or looking at her funny. Maybe she should have gone with Cora to the local bar the rodeo crowd had taken over. Josephine clearly needed to relax if she was scaring everyone away.

But she'd been feeling out of sorts and antisocial since she'd left Silas's trailer that morning. She'd worried he'd come find her, to ask why she'd left.

He hadn't.

Which worried her more.

Where was Cora when she needed her?

Josephine pulled Comet from his stall and looped the lead rope around one of the bars and got to work replacing the thrown shoe.

Comet dozed while she rasped the bottom of the hoof flat

and drove in the first two nails. His head popped up the same time Josephine heard Cora's laugh in the distance.

Cora's laughs were always loud and as infectious as an STD at a porn convention. Josephine glanced up and Cora turned the corner at the top of the aisle. Josephine waved her over.

Cora said goodbye to her friends and jogged up, the fringe on her long sleeves bouncing with each step.

Josephine dropped Comet's hoof and slipped the hammer into the loop on her chaps. "Just the wom—"

"Why the hell didn't you tell me you slept with Foss?" Cora didn't have an inside voice. Or discretion.

People passing by slowed and stared before walking on again.

"Would you keep your voice down?"

"Doesn't matter. Everyone already knew about it but me."

"You were asleep when I got in. I didn't want to wake you. Besides, I thought you were staying the night with—"

Cora waved a dismissive hand. "That's over." Cora didn't look all broken up about it. She looked her normal, brushed out, made up, perfectly dressed self. "And don't change the subject."

Josephine stretched Comet's leg back and settled his hoof over her thigh and started tapping in the rest of the nails. "I guess that rumor accounts for all the weird looks I've been getting all day."

Cora settled on a bale of hay across from Comet's stall. "It's true, then."

Around a couple of nails she had sticking out of her mouth, Josephine said, "Of course it's not true."

She pounded the last nail home, twisted off the ends, clenched them tight and gave Comet back his hoof. That shoe wasn't coming off anytime soon.

"So that redhead on the flag team was lying when she said she saw you sneaking out of Silas's trailer at dawn?" Cora chewed on a stalk of hay, one booted foot on the bale, and a you-can-tell-me-the-truth smile on her face.

Rodeo rumors flew faster than Telex, faster even than her hometown gossip grannies. Which said a lot.

Josephine started gathering up her tools. She needed to set the record straight. Did it make her bad that a small, tiny, minuscule, fraction of herself wished the rumors were true? "Yes, I came out of Silas's trailer at dawn. But no, I didn't have sex with him. I didn't even sleep with him. Now I'm tired and grouchy and—"

"Horny."

Josephine couldn't hold back the bubble of laughter as heat rose on her cheeks.

"I knew you couldn't go the whole season without someone tickling your fancy."

"Tickling my fancy? Now you're starting to sound like my grandmother."

"Hey, Cora, get your sweet ass over here." The deep male voice came from about ten stalls away. It wasn't the roper Cora had left with last night.

Cora's grin expanded, and her eyes lit as she started backing down the aisle. "You should listen to your grandmother. She's a smart woman. All my grandmother gave me when I left on the circuit was a container of oatmeal cookies. Yours gave you a box of condoms and an order not to dare come back until they were gone."

"I'm pretty certain that's not normal."

"Doesn't make it bad advice."

———

BACK AT THE CALGARY RODEO GROUNDS AFTER A FEW BEERS AT the local bar with his best friend and fellow bull rider Tobias

Navarro, Silas climbed out of Toby's rusted out, beater of a truck that burned oil faster than gas. A cloud of exhaust gathered around Silas's boots from a crack in the pipes, tickling the back of his throat.

"You should put some ice on that." Toby flicked a finger toward the new bruise blooming on the right side of Silas's jaw.

Funny. Needing to ice a bruise was what had gotten him the new one. "Yeah, I'll jump right on that." The words were right, but his tone said *screw that*.

"Don't let Monte and Chet get to you. No matter what gets back to Cox, the man doesn't have near the pull with the circuit that he used to. Besides that, you didn't do anything wrong. Shake it off and concentrate on your ride."

"Sure." Toby had a point. Though the sinking feeling that Silas had painted a neon target on his back by getting involved with Josephine wouldn't go away.

Silas leaned his hands on the door sill and Toby said, "And buddy, next time, hit them with your left hand. Hard to make Cheyenne if your grip hand's busted."

Silas tapped his open hand on the roof of the truck cab and backed away. "Asshole."

Toby whooped out a laugh and left Silas in a choking cloud of exhaust. He wiped blood off his scuffed knuckles and flexed and extended his right hand. At least his grip didn't feel bad.

He zig-zagged through all the rigs and detoured by Josephine's trailer on his way to his truck, but no one was home. He hadn't seen her since she'd slipped out of his camper the morning before. He'd been hanging out—make that *hiding* out —at the bar.

It wasn't because of the rumors, which hopefully that fight had squashed. It wasn't because he was embarrassed, and it certainly wasn't because he didn't want to see her.

It was because he wanted to see her too much.

He wanted to talk to her, put his hands on her, and do everything those rumors said they'd done.

And then some.

But that was the problem. She'd been the one concerned about losing focus and he hadn't taken her seriously.

Now she was all he could think about at a time when he needed laser focus. Cheyenne was only a handful of rodeos away, and he and Toby and Monte and that skinny kid named Freeman were in a tight earnings race to make the final cutoff. Depending on how the other men's rides went meant he was only a buck-off, or a lousy score away from not qualifying.

He'd tried to stay away from Josephine. But that had only made his focus worse.

So now he'd see what would happen when he didn't stay away.

Silas came around the corner of a stock trailer and stopped short. The door to his camper stood wide open, Monte standing in the doorway. "Get the hell out of my truck."

Monte clump-clumped down the steps more like he owned the place and less like a thief on the run. Monte reached behind him and pulled some folded bills off the top of Silas's rig bag. "I was just leaving you the money I owed for the gas from last week."

Silas snagged the money from Monte's hands. "You could have given it to me at the bar."

"Didn't get the chance." Monte had a small cut near his left brow where the skin had split under the impact of Silas's fist.

Silas shoved the money in his pocket and as a parting shot said, "Stay away."

Monte put his hands up in mock surrender and backed up a couple of steps before turning and walking away. Silas scanned the trailer and checked the hidden compartment where he'd stashed all his winnings, but everything was undisturbed and all his money accounted for. He changed into his riding jeans and chaps and grabbed his bullrope and the rest of his gear and headed to the warm-up arenas. He needed to find Josephine and apologize.

At the third arena, he found her lazy loping the barrel pattern. As she approached the third barrel, Silas could already tell her angle was off and her turn too tight as she came around. Comet rammed Josephine's knee into the barrel, dumping it in the dirt.

A kid ran across the arena and set it back up for her, dodging other warm-up riders as he ran in and out. Silas folded his arms over the top rail of the fence. Josephine and Comet were almost to the fence when she glanced up and noticed him there. She pulled Comet up short and the gelding tossed his head at the sudden bit contact.

She scratched at his withers. "Sorry, buddy." To Silas, she said, "Hey."

"Hey." That was about as smooth as arena dirt after a rodeo. "Look, uh..."

"What happened to your face?"

"Had to set a someone straight about the rumor. My fault. I should have walked you back to your trailer the other night. I forget sometimes how fast the rumors fly." He pointed to his jaw. "I think I put an end to it, if that helps."

"I don't care so much about the rumors unless it gets back to my father. Let me guess, Chet?"

And Monte. And some dude who'd had too much whiskey and just wanted to fight. All of them had been lucky the bar owner had kicked them out and hadn't called the cops. "Does it matter?"

"No." She hitched a thumb over her shoulder toward the barrel. "I should probably get back to it. My timing needs a little adjustment."

"Comet knows the pattern and his job. Maybe you need to relax coming into that barrel. Not take things so seriously." By the way her expression darkened, the advice wasn't welcomed.

"Hah. Relax. Easy for you to say. You're winning. You have money in the bank. If you don't finish in the money in Cheyenne, you just move on to the indoor rodeos come fall. You don't have to crawl home to daddy."

"Neither do you."

"I'm barely covering expenses. Sometimes I have to sneak into the beer tent just to score a free hot dog because I had to choose between feeding myself or my horse. Besides, I made a promise."

"Break it." He didn't say *for him,* but that was implied.

She side-passed Comet to the fence. "What are you saying?"

He stepped on the bottom rail, not knowing how to answer. He only knew that he didn't want to have to say goodbye come Cheyenne. "I've got last draw tonight."

"I've got first. I could maybe find a seat by the chutes, after."

"And I could watch you from the alleyway, before."

She smiled and settled deep in the saddle. Comet let out a heavy sigh. "Okay. It's a date then. I mean not a date just a time for us to be together but not together because we will be riding but—"

"Hotstuff. It's a date."

Her grin widened, exposing a dimple he didn't know she had.

"I gotta go." He leaned across the top of the fence, his face inches from hers. "But I think you should give me a kiss before I do."

"For good luck?" Comet cocked a hip, shifting her closer. Silas would have to find a carrot for his wingman.

"That, and if everyone is going to talk, we might as well give them something to talk about."

That adorable dimple reappeared as she closed the gap between them and pressed her lips to his. She broke the quick kiss, but he caught her with a hand behind her neck. "That's not going to cut it."

Her narrowed eyes said *challenge-accepted* and she leaned into the kiss. He angled his head, taking the kiss deeper. He tasted the tamale on her tongue and smelled the hay in her hair. His heart beat in that crazy rhythm he got right before he rode, and he couldn't get enough. His loose jeans got tight and the top rail cut into his groin. Comet edged away, and when Silas couldn't lean over any further, he let her go. "See you at the chutes."

She pointed Comet for the first barrel. "I'll see you in the alley."

———

THE STANDS WERE PACKED BY THE TIME SILAS MADE IT TO THE chutes. The air sizzled with electric excitement, and the light breeze mixed the dark smells of dirt and dander, beer and bratwurst, cotton candy and cow patty. The adrenaline seeped into his system making the arena lights brighter, the raucous cheers louder.

Over the PA they announced the rodeo clowns as they came out. The crowd went wild. Silas looked up from adjusting his rope because from the crowd's reaction he was positive Jesus had just walked on water or Elvis Presley had walked on stage. But no, Rowdy Boyd had run into the arena, waving his hat in the air. Off to the left a woman screamed and held up a poster that said *Rowdy Boyd, I want to have your baby.*

For a guy like Rowdy, that was a monstrous promotion from wannabe bull rider to celebrity bullfighter. Everyone had seen the news footage of the recent saves he'd made. The media and female attention were well deserved, and only a couple of assholes dared give him crap anymore for not making it in one of the most dangerous sports in the world.

When it was his turn, the spotter said to Silas, "You're up."

The big gray Brahman jostled and jumped and kicked in the chute. His tail flicked feces, spray painting the inside of the rails with fresh manure. Silas climbed over the top rail, balanced over the bull and looked into the stands where the wives and the fiancés and the girlfriends of the competitors sat. He scanned the seats, but he didn't see Josephine any—

There.

In the corner, by herself, as if unsure where she fit in with those women. Where she fit in with him. She gave a little wave when she caught his eye. He nodded back, then sat down on fifteen hundred pounds of hide and horn and raw power. His heart hit that awkward, crazy rhythm it always hit, except this time when he got on the bull, he wasn't thinking about the ride, he was thinking about that kiss.

While he adjusted his rope, he was thinking about that dimple.

When he wrapped the tail of the rope around his hand, he was thinking about the sweet, sweet curve of her ass.

And as he settled into his rope and nodded his head, he pictured the perfect ride, how hot and wet and tight she would be as he sank balls deep into her warmth.

His cow bells clacked and clanked as the bull jumped free of the chute, landing with a jarring stride that shorted his spine by a foot and knocked his kidneys into his throat.

The bull spun to the left, Silas's spur catching in the thick hide, but he was already off balance and behind the movement. His shoulder strained and his trick elbow made that popping sound. One spin, two spin, three. Silas's mind caught up with the ride and he felt that hesitation, that bunching of muscle beneath the hide, and he knew the next spin would be to the right.

He went with the movement, his left arm high overhead for balance. It should have hurt his ribs like hell, but it didn't.

He whooped as his internal clock counted down the seconds.

He would make the bell. In three, two, o—

A head flip, a nasty belly roll, and beneath him where there had been a bull there was only air. He was aware of three things as he sailed across the arena like a human cannonball—the crowd went quiet, the buzzer went off, and the rope was still wrapped around his hand.

He ducked his head, and tried to roll out of the fall, but he landed hard on his shoulder, the back of his head smacking against dirt. It didn't matter how deep the dirt was, it was never soft enough.

Pain shot through his head as his brain played bumper cars with his skull. The stands went blurry, then starry, then black. All he heard was the beat of his heart behind his eardrums, not a thud, thud, thundering, but a great galloping in the distance.

Far, far, far, awa—

5
____

THE DOOR TO THE WAITING ROOM AT THE HOSPITAL OPENED AND an older man in a white coat and a put-out expression walked in. Josephine stood, knowing he came for her, not because he knew who she was, but because someone on the hospital's board of directors owed her father a favor.

"Can I see him now?" Josephine asked the doctor.

The doctor opened his mouth to say something, then must have thought better of it. As much as she liked to deny she was Caine Cox daughter, sometimes it paid to be her as well. Not that this favor from her father would come without repercussions when she got home, but that was weeks away and she would worry about that later.

The doctor turned to leave and said, "Follow me."

Her boots echoed in the hall as she jogged to keep up with the doctor's brutal pace. "How is he? Is he awake? Is he talking? Is anything broken? Is—"

The doctor stopped abruptly, and she almost ran into the back of him. He turned and said, "I've been ordered to allow you into his room. But since you're not his wife, nor his next of kin, his medical condition isn't up for discussion."

"Yeah, yeah. Okay. Fine. Just take me to him."

Two doors later, the doctor turned the knob and led her into the room. The overhead lights were off, the blinds on the window drawn. A soft light from the fixture over the bed was enough to see the easy rise and fall of Silas's chest.

She approached the bed, and reached out to take his hand, hesitated.

"You can touch him." The doctor lost the edge to his tone.

She glanced up. "Will he wake soon?"

The doctor gave her a look that said that was something he couldn't discuss, but then he said, "Everything indicates that he should. But this is a brain we're dealing with, so we'll have to wait and see."

"Can he hear me?"

"I don't know. Now if you'll excuse me."

The doctor left, and she pulled a chair by the bed and sat. The heart monitor beat a steady, soothing rhythm. Silas's color was good, and if he didn't have the white bandage around his head, she'd think he was only sleeping. Reaching out, she took his hand in both of hers. He was warm, and alive, and it made her eyes sting.

She hadn't known what she'd expected, but feeling the warmth, knowing his heart beat and his blood pulsed, broke the tension in her chest that had prevented her from taking in a full breath since the bull had launched him into the air.

Seconds turned to minutes. Minutes turned to hours. The nurse came in and took vitals. The doctor came by on his rounds. Silas remained unconscious through it all. The halls quieted down as visiting hours ended. Thanks again to her father, no one asked her to leave. Her eyes drifted closed and she caught herself nodding off.

"Go. Get some sleep."

Silas. His voice held a tremor, and if the room hadn't been silent except for the faint beep of the heart monitor, she wouldn't have heard him.

"You're awake." The knot of tension in her shoulders eased and her stomach climbed off the floor. "Let me go get the nurse."

She stood to leave, but he didn't let go of her hand. "Hang on."

"But they said—"

"Sit. Talk to me." He found the controls and buzzed the head of his bed up. "What's the damage?" He glanced down at the IV in his left hand. Wiggled his legs under the covers. "Seems like everything works."

"They wouldn't discuss your medical care with me, but I don't think anything is broken. Just a bad concussion from what I can figure out."

He reached up and ran his fingers over the bandage, poking gingerly until he hit a sore spot on the back of his head. He grimaced and dropped his hand to his lap. "Good thing I've got a hard head."

"And you said there's no bad juju. You were very lucky. You could have—"

"Being dumped wasn't bad juju. It was my fault. I let myself get distracted."

He didn't add the *by you* indicating what had distracted him, but the way he looked at her, she knew. Which made her feel guilty and giddy all at the same time.

"Did you win?"

"What?"

"Your run. You know where you get on your horse and you gallop around these big barrels."

Not even close. That's why you had to focus. That's why you didn't get involved with men on the circuit. "Cora got second." At least one of them had money now.

Silas's voice was getting stronger and stronger, but he still sounded froggy. Josephine handed him some water. He drank. "What happened? You two looked great out there."

"I just…" Had been thinking about him waiting for her in the alley when she was finished. It should have made her faster. It hadn't. "We were just off tonight."

"I'm sorry." He rubbed a hand over his forehead, and his guard dropped, and she saw how much pain he was in.

"Let me get that nurse."

He nodded and relaxed back against the pillow. Josephine was almost to the door when he said, "Was it my fault?"

"Was what your fault?"

"You not winning. Did my being in the alley—"

She didn't want him to know how much he affected her. She plastered on an indulgent smile. "You must have hit your head harder than I thought. You're talking nonsense."

His eyes fluttered and drifted closed, but he said, "Cheyenne is just—"

"Yeah, I know. I'm good."

He fought the heaviness in his lids, but beneath the disappointment on his face, she thought she'd detected a hint of a smile. "I think you should get that nurse now. Oh, and Josephine?"

"Yeah?"

"Thanks for coming."

———

THE NURSE CAME IN AND KICKED JOSEPHINE OUT INTO THE HALL despite Silas's protests. Vitals were checked, and questions asked, and then the doctor came in and rechecked what the nurses had checked, repeated the same questions then tried to scorch his retinas with a penlight.

The bright light made his head pound harder. If he hadn't known better, he'd have thought a bull was stomping his skull into the ground. He closed his eyes, but minutes later he still saw stars behind his lids.

Someone squeezed his shoulder. "Mr. Foss?" The nurse, he supposed, but he didn't open his eyes to be certain. "The doctor was talking to you."

Silas shook his head to try to dislodge some of the fuzzy wool that made his thinking slow. *Ouch.* He clamped a hand to his head, wanting to curl up into a ball and roll away from the pain. "What doc?"

"I said we want to keep you for a few days for observation and monitor you for any brain swelling or hemorrhage and—"

Silas sat up, his head spun, and he had to balance himself with both hands. "I'm not staying."

He didn't have time for that. More importantly, he didn't have the money for that. Getting medical insurance as a bull rider wasn't easy. Or cheap. As it was, he'd be lucky if this extended nap didn't drain what funds he had in the bank. He and Toby would never save enough money for a roughstock ranch at this rate.

Hands grabbed his shoulders and tried to push him back down.

Silas stilled and leveled a don't-fuck-with-me glare at the doctor. "Let me go."

"You can't go in there." The woman's voice came from somewhere down the hall. High pitched, angry. "I'm going to call security—"

"Be my guest, sweetheart." Toby rounded the corner of Silas's room, followed by Josephine, Cora and a nurse who had more steam coming out of her ears than a cartoon bull.

"Find my clothes." Silas slipped off the edge of the bed. His feet didn't hit hard, but the landing jarred his head enough that his knees buckled, and he had to catch himself on the bed rail.

"What are you doing?" Josephine grabbed his arm. "Get back in bed."

Cold air hit his naked ass, but he couldn't find a reason to care. He started taking off the gown. He was getting dressed with or without anyone's help.

"Out." The doctor started waving his hand like a traffic cop sending a line of cars through a red light. "Everyone out."

The nurses ushered his friends out of the room, closing the door firmly behind them. She crossed her arms over her chest in front of the door as if he'd have to go through her to get out. The doctor, he could take, but the nurse was a substantial woman who looked like she nibbled on razors for fun. In his current condition, Silas didn't like his chances.

He collapsed on the side of the bed. More because his legs were shaking from the strain than because he'd decided to follow the doctor's orders. For the next fifteen to twenty minutes, he and the doctor negotiated what he was and wasn't willing to do. Finally, they had a plan, and the nurse allowed his friends back into the room.

"What's the verdict?" Toby was the first to speak. "Are they letting you go or do I have to come back at midnight with a posse to break you out?"

"I'm leaving," Silas said.

"Against medical advice." The resignation in the doctor's voice reminded Silas of his mother after she'd realized she couldn't stop him from riding bulls. The doctor finished signing something on Silas's record and handed it to the nurse. "And under certain conditions."

"I can't ride next weekend, so I'm going to miss Salinas." Saying those words left a bitter taste on his tongue that made Silas want to spit. "And I have to stay within a ten-minute drive of the hospital for the next four days in case I have any complications."

"That'll still give you plenty of time to meet up with us in Ogden," Josephine said.

"And he can't be alone or drive for at least a week." The doctor wasn't helping.

The smile on Toby's face crumbled. They were travel partners and even though Toby now had his own ride, they still caravanned together. They had each other's backs. "Uh... I drew a bad bull for Salinas and like my chances better in Rock Springs." Toby glanced first at Josephine and then almost desperately at Cora. "I can stay a day. Maybe. But then I gotta go, buddy."

"No problem." No way was Silas gonna be the reason Toby missed out on a chance to ride at the Big Daddy. "You gotta do what you gotta do on the road to Cheyenne. I'll make do and catch up with you when I can."

Josephine stepped forward. "I'll stay with you."

If he couldn't ask his best friend to stay, he certainly couldn't ask his...his... he didn't quite know what to call her, but considering what he wanted to do to her, with her, he couldn't exactly call her his *friend*. "That won't be necessary. I'll stick close to the hospital." He glanced at the doctor. "That'll have to be good enough."

"I'm staying." Josephine crossed her arms and raised her brows at him as if daring him to argue.

"Fine." As much as he hated the idea of her missing a rodeo, he loved the idea of four days alone with her.

"Glad that's settled. See you in Ogden." Toby clapped him on the shoulder and started backing out of the room. Silas knew Toby needed to pack up and get on the road. Toby turned back at the door and said, "And buddy, if it makes you feel any better, I think that you flying off the bull got Rowdy laid again. He should probably thank you for helping out his sex life."

THREE DAYS.

Three days of keeping his hands to himself when all Silas wanted to do was make Josephine his.

Three days of falling for her laughs and her smiles and her brains when he knew it would be best for his career if he stayed away, and three days of hoping like hell she wouldn't come to her senses and leave his sorry ass in Calgary.

"Well?" Silas sat slumped on the converted bed in his camper's dinette area, his bare feet plopped in Josephine's lap on the far end, his head resting on a stack of pillows as he glared at her over the tops of his cards.

"Don't rush me." Her eyes cut from her cards to him then back to her cards. If this were a high stakes poker game, he wouldn't want to be betting against her.

"Either you have an Ace, or you don't."

"Fine." She took a slow sip of five-dollar-a-bottle wine from one of the Dixie cups they'd stolen from the closed concession stand and folded her cards. Her eyes cut to his. Right before she spoke, he saw triumph toy with her lips. "Go fish."

"You're lying." He held out his hand for her cards, but she pulled them to her chest.

"Stop being a sore loser."

"Sore loser? I'm not the one who faked a paper cut when launching my paper airplane off the top of the bleachers and insisted on a do-over." He pulled his feet from her lap and sat up, glad that the simple movement didn't send his head spinning anymore.

"The cut was little and hard to see. Those hurt the worst."

He held out his hand again, unable to keep the smile at bay. "The cards. Lemme see."

She held them out of his reach.

"Last chance."

"Oooooh. What's the big bad bull rider gonna—"

He dove to her side of the bed. Josephine let out a noise, part laugh, part screech. It made his ears ring, and his heart skitter sideways. His heart had been doing that a lot lately. Maybe the ER doctor had gotten it all wrong. Maybe his head was fine, but the fall had damaged his heart.

He straddled her legs and grabbed at the cards. Even with her arms straining to keep the cards away from him, she was no match for his long reach. He gripped her wrist, her pulse galloping beneath the tips of his fingers.

Her laughter died as her gaze locked on his lips. *Hell.*

Having to nurse his concussion when all he'd wanted to do was roll her beneath him was worse than having his hand caught in the bullrope and being dragged across the arena.

He wanted to sink into her until he forgot he couldn't ride this weekend, until Silas forgot his shot at Cheyenne was slipping through his fingers, and before he remembered Josephine's father still had the power and the pull to jeopardize his career.

He'd climbed the bleachers that morning without getting a migraine. A little romp in the trailer couldn't be any worse.

He released her wrist no longer caring about the cards, and brushed the pad of his thumb over her bottom lip.

"What are you doing?" She asked.

"I'm going to kiss you and work my way down from there."

"The doctor said not to overexert yourself."

"I'm fine."

She pushed against his chest. "Lay down."

"I'm not five. I don't need to l—"

She grabbed the hem of his T-shirt and stripped it off his

body. The quick movement made the bruising on his side ache, but the pain barely had time to register before the heat in her eyes made his blood rush south, with a roar and a whoosh like a drain being pulled on Niagara Falls.

"Lay back," she said again.

"Yes, ma'am." Silas settled back, resting his weight on his elbows to watch Josephine crawl over the top of him. The scoop neck of her tank top sagged, gracing him with a view of the most jaw dropping cleavage on the circuit.

He reached out to her, but she shook her head and gave him that same disappointed look his kindergarten teacher had had when he'd refused to color inside the lines. With a hand in the middle of his chest, she pushed him back into the cushion. His damp skin stuck to the Naugahyde. She straddled his hips and reached above him, her breasts inches from his face as she dropped her cards on the counter behind his head.

He wanted to rise, to claim one glorious mound with his mouth and then the other, but that would be getting way ahead of themselves. Yes, they'd kissed. Yes, everything she'd done to this point said she was interested, but she wasn't one who played the field. He wanted her to set the pace.

She sat, her knees straddling his hips, and he skimmed his hands up her bare thighs, over her shorts, and settled them at her waist. Around his ribs where the purples of his bruise had faded to greens and yellows, she traced the outline with her finger. He flinched, and she snatched her hand back.

"That hurt?"

"It's managable." It wasn't an out and out lie. But he wanted to push the ack-what-have-I-done look off her face. "You could kiss it and make it better."

The mischievous curve of her lips raised goosebumps on his flesh and made him harder. He wanted to grab her hips and grind against her, but he folded his arms behind his head and gave her full, unbridled access.

"If you don't think it will make it worse." Without waiting for his answer, she leaned forward and pressed her lips to his side, and his goosebumps doubled in size. She worked her way over his rib cage, bracing herself on one hand while the other skimmed over the ridges and valleys of his abdomen. His blood pressure spiked, and his pulse kicked up, the *thump-trump* echoing in his bruise and at his temples, but no way would he stop her sweet torture.

She laved a line from his ribs, over his pectoral muscle and to the flat of his nipple. His eyes closed, and he brought a hand to the back of her head and held her in place. It sent a tug and a tingle to his groin and forced a groan from his lips.

"Come here." He cupped her face and brought her mouth to his. She tasted of cheap wine, and even though she hadn't touched a horse in days, he caught a whiff of sweet hay in her hair as if she'd rolled naked in the cool grass, her skin warmed by the Canadian summer sun.

Her kiss was light, tentative. Silas ran his hands under her shirt and hugged her to him. She moaned. Soft. Encouraging. She fell into the kiss, her tongue dueling with his.

Before he'd given it conscious thought, he reversed their positions. The movement tugged at his ribs and made his head spin. Dots appeared in his peripheral vision, but when she'd murmured his name with a naked rawness that boiled his blood, he wasn't convinced the concussion was entirely to blame for his lightheadedness.

She pulled back from the kiss. Their breath mixing in harsh pants that made ribs hurt and his chest ache.

Placing a hand on his cheek, she said, "You okay? I think maybe we should stop."

"Think again." He dipped his head, going in for another kiss.

Was that her way of trying to put the brakes on? His next words were going to be painful to say, but he said them anyway. "Unless you want to stop."

"No." Her answer came quick. No stutter. No hesitation. No embarrassment. He had to admire a woman who knew what she wanted and wasn't afraid to say so.

He settled between her legs, bracing his weight on his elbows, his arousal at the juncture of her thighs. Her hands went to his ass, and she arched up against him. "Please tell me you have condoms," she said.

"Hang on." He pushed up with one hand and reached up over the counter, feeling around until he'd found what he wanted. His arm shook under his weight, his strength nowhere near where it should be.

He settled down beside her, her cards in his hand as he fanned them out. "I knew you had an ace."

"You sneak." She laughed and socked him in the arm. "If all that was a rouse to see my cards, I'm gonna—"

He shut her up with a kiss. She took the cards from his hand and tossed them over his shoulder. The cards fluttered to the floor. At midday, even with all the windows open, the inside of the camper was getting steamy.

Silas broke the kiss. "Hold that thought." Sweat slicked his skin as he stripped out of his sweat pants.

Josephine tossed her clothes to the floor, where they landed with a soft *whump*. She lay there on his bed, bare before him, except for the not-so-innocent smile on her face. She reached out to him, but if he didn't grab a condom now, he knew he'd be hard-pressed to do it later.

"I'll be right back. Don't go anywhere."

"I'm not exactly dressed for travel."

He pawed through a couple of drawers. Where the hell was that box? Drawer after drawer, cabinet after cabinet he searched and searched. Josephine sighed, and he glanced behind him. She'd rolled onto her belly, her head resting on her folded hands with her delectable ass face up, taunting him.

If he couldn't find his supply... "You wouldn't happen to have—"

"Yeah. I've got condoms. In my trailer. Which is in Salinas with Cora about now."

6

———————

"See," Josephine said. "Bad juju. I'm telling you. This season is cursed."

"I don't think my inability to find a box of condoms supports your theory of bad juju on the circuit. I'm pretty sure the cosmos doesn't care if we get laid. This is more of an organizational problem."

"Maybe."

Silas was bent over, digging through a bottom drawer. She reached a hand out, wanting to grab that bodacious chunk of cowboy bootie.

"Aha, found them." Silas turned around brandishing a brand new box of condoms in his hand.

Josephine scooted back, making room for him on the bed. While he'd been searching for the condoms, she'd re-tucked the sheet around the cushions. Nothing worse than sweaty skin on Naugahyde.

He grabbed his head and leaned against the counter, the box of condoms clattering to the floor. This was a bad idea. She scrambled off the bed and took him by the hand. "Lay down before you fall down."

He didn't argue. He half-fell, half-rolled onto the bed. When Josephine went to grab her clothes, Silas clasped her wrist. "What do you think you're doing?"

"You're not in any shape to—"

"Look at me. All of me. Tell me I'm not ready for this." His words came out low, but steady.

She looked him over, from the determination in his eyes to the pulse-pounding at the base of his throat, to the taut muscles of his body to the impressive erection at the juncture of his thighs.

When her eyes met his again, he said, "I'm ready."

He rolled onto his stomach and snagged the box off the floor and handed it to her. She fiddled with the box. Wanting to rip it open but not wishing to participate in anything that would hurt him either. The doctor did leave him with strict instructions not to overexert himself for the next week.

As if he read her mind, he took the box from her hand, ripped a packet open and sheathed himself. He reached out a hand to her. "Come here."

She took it but didn't step forward when he tugged. "Under one condition."

"Name it."

Even as he said it, his hand went to his forehead. This was a horrible idea. But it didn't stop Josephine from saying, "I do all the work."

"Deal." His grin said *this ought to be fun.*

He pulled her onto the bed, and she straddled his thighs, taking him in her hands and guiding him to her entrance. "You sure?"

He let out a groan, surging up until he'd buried himself balls deep. Josephine blew out a breath, a smile on her lips as she adjusted to his breadth. *Holy guacamole.*

When she started to move, he gripped her hips and said, "Give me a minute."

"I knew this was a bad—" She started to climb off but his hold on her only tightened.

"I'm fine. My head's fine. At least the big one is." He huffed out a heavy breath. "Sweet baby Jesus, you're tight." His jaw clenched, and this time when he groaned, she knew it wasn't because of the concussion.

She started slow, increasing the rhythm and the pleasure. When Silas tried matching her, stroke for mindblowing stroke, she stilled.

He opened his eyes, his lids heavy with lust. "What's wrong?"

"I'm supposed to be doing all the work. You are supposed to be laying there and enjoying it."

"I am enj—"

"Stop moving."

"You're killin'—"

"Hands above your head." She leaned forward, her breasts smushing against his chest as she pinned his wrists together with her hand. "If you move, I'll have to get a rope."

"Promise?"

When she went to sit back up, his arms came around her back and held her against him. She opened her mouth to protest, but then he rolled his hips and drove up into her, driving every word, every sentence, every thought from her mind until all she was surviving on was instinct and passion.

He drove faster and harder, their bodies slick and sliding together as the temperature in the camper climbed to combustible levels. Josephine's heart clattered in her chest, her blood rushing, racing as he ravaged her body. His breath, harsh pants in her ear. His steady rhythm now hard, erratic.

He was close. She was close. They were so very, very close.

She buried her head in his shoulder, nipping at the tender

skin. He reached between them, gliding his fingers through her folds, catching that bundle of nerves. One touch, one brush, one nudge, and she fell off the cliff.

No. She didn't fall.

She jumped.

And took him with her.

He held her tight as the aftershocks wracked their bodies. His hands cupping her ass as he gently thrust inside her, not wanting it to end, to be over.

His fingers trailed up the muscles on either side of her spine, sending shivers through her body, and tightening her around him. His breath caught. He cupped her face, and tilted his head back, looking her in the eyes.

The heat of embarrassment rushed up her cheeks, and she glanced away. Not because she was ashamed of what they'd shared, but because of the way his gaze laid her bare. As if he could see all that she was, and more importantly, all that she wasn't.

"Look at me," he said.

She did. It wasn't easy looking into the eyes of a man who looked like he'd found his forever when she knew, *knew*, forever wasn't what she wanted. At least not anytime soon.

"You know this is temporary, right cowboy? That when Cheyenne is over I have to go back home—"

"All I ask is here and now. One day at a time. That's what we'd agreed. Right?"

She nodded because her throat had closed and the words wouldn't come.

He brushed her damp hair from her face and pressed a kiss to her forehead and pulled her in tight. "That's my girl."

Bam, bam, bam.

The camper door shuddered. Josephine startled and tried to scramble off him, but Silas held her tighter.

"Go away," Silas hollered.

Bam, bam, bam. Bam, bam, bam. Bam, bam, bam.

"Open up, Foss."

"Chet." Josephine bit out the word like a bitter curse. Why was he still here?

"Stay here." Silas rolled from beneath her and ditched the condom. He yanked on his sweatpants, staggered a step, then caught himself.

"*Foss.*"

Silas opened the door, blocking her view with his body and barked out a "What?"

Silas sagged against the door jamb, and Josephine scrambled to get on her clothes. They shouldn't have had sex. Silas clearly wasn't fully recovered.

"Josephine in there?" Chet said.

Silas had told her to stay put, but it wasn't any secret she was in Silas's camper. She'd been in it since he'd gotten out of the hospital. She fought with her bra, then gave up, pulling her tank top over her head as Silas said, "You know she is."

"I need to talk to her."

"Don't you have something better to do than hang around Calgary scratching your nuts?"

Josephine was a grown woman. She didn't need Silas to protect her from Chet. She came up beside Silas and opened the door wider. A straw cowboy hat shaded Chet's eyes from the midday sun. He had a hardness to his expression that said he would gladly go a few rounds with Silas if given a chance.

Chet's eyes narrowed at Silas. "I go where she goes. Cox's orders."

Josephine wrapped her arm around Silas's waist. "What do you want, Chet?"

"Your father's on the phone at the arena office. The long-distance call is costing him a fortune, you should—"

"You can tell my father—"

"It's your mother." Chet caught the door as Josephine started to close it. "Something's happened."

———

Josephine paced the office at the Calgary rodeo arena, stretching the long phone cord to its limits as she ping-ponged between the back wall and the front window.

"It's your mother." Her father's voice had an edge. It always had an edge. Usually anger or frustration or authority or any number of things. Usually none of them pleasant.

But this edge, this tone, she'd never heard before.

She gripped the phone tighter as her gut twisted and crashed back on itself. "W-What happened?"

Silas caught her as she passed by and she allowed him to tuck her under his arm. She could hear her father breathing on the other end of the phone, but no words came.

Chet stood in the corner of the office, staring at the floor, his hat in his hands. Giving her as much privacy as he could without actually leaving the room.

"Is she dead?"

Still nothing from the other end. Had she said those words aloud or had she just said them in her head?

Her father cleared his throat. "She's at the hospital in ICU. She had a stroke."

Josephine's world tilted, her knees gave way, and Silas eased her to the ground beneath the window. "I'm on my way. Or send me a ticket, and I can be there later today."

"No."

"What do you mean? I'm not staying—"

"Finish the circuit. Finish in Cheyenne. Get that foolishness out of your system, then come home where you belong. Where you'll stay. The doctors say your mother's recovery will be long and arduous. You'll be needed at the ranch."

"But I—"

"Don't argue with me, Josephine. For once in your damn life, don't argue with me. If you had been home, if you had called, if you hadn't worried your mother for days and weeks and months—"

"Whoa, wait." The roar in Josephine's ears eased as her heart tumbled in her chest. Her head went fuzzy and her vision blurred. Did her father just say what she thought he'd said? "Are...are you saying this is my fault?"

There was no answer from the other end. "Hello, hello? You still there?" Still nothing. "Dad?"

"I'll see you after Cheyenne."

The line went dead, and Josephine slumped against the wall. Her fault. Her father thought her mother's stroke was all her fault.

Funny how her father didn't think her mother's stroke had anything to do with the fact that she refused to take care of herself, to eat healthy, to take her blood pressure and blood sugar meds. No. According to her father, none of that had anything to do with her mother's stroke.

It was all *her* fault.

And as much as she knew that wasn't true, that knowledge didn't do anything to soothe her guilt. Because she did know how her mother worried and stressed when Josephine was gone. She knew that her mother combated her stress by baking, and then by eating.

No Josephine wasn't entirely to blame, but by following the circuit, by following her dreams, she hadn't made her mother's life any easier.

Josephine thumped the back of her head against the wood

paneling again and again. Not hard enough to really hurt, but hard enough to dull the massive onslaught of emotions.

"Hey now." Silas placed his hand behind her head to soften the blows. He plopped down on the floor beside her, curling her into his chest. To Chet, he said, "Give us a minute."

By the scowl on Chet's face, Josephine thought Chet was about to say no, but he snugged his hat down low on his head and reached for the office door. He stopped with his hand on the knob and over his shoulder said, "Sorry about your momma, Josephine."

"Th—" Josephine cleared her throat. It felt like she'd swallowed a bucket full of cockleburs. "Thank you."

After Chet left, Silas said, "You want to tell me about it, or do you want to be alone?"

"Yes."

Silas chuckled at Josephine's inconsistent answer. "Why don't you start by filling me in and then you can have your space if you need that."

There wasn't much to tell, so it didn't take long. Josephine pushed her emotions aside, kept her explanation to the basics. She didn't know how to express her conflicted feelings, so she didn't even try.

When she'd finished, Silas let out a breath. "Look, family obligations are tough. It's understandable that your father would want you at home—"

"You think that's okay that he gets to unilaterally decide what I do with my life? You think that I should give up my dreams, my—"

"That's not what I'm saying at all." Silas took her by the shoulders, gave her a gentle shake. "You didn't let me finish."

"Sorry." She stared at the ground. His concern and frustration too raw in his eyes.

He put his arm around her and planted a kiss on the side of

her head. "This is your life. You get to decide what'll make you happy. You and no one else. But you also must balance that with what's best for your family. I know that's not telling you anything you don't already know. I'm just saying I'm sure you can find a compromise that makes everyone happy. If you can't, then you at least have to come to terms with that decision. You matter, Josephine. Your happiness matters. Don't ever lose sight of that."

Josephine nodded because those cockleburs were stubborn and weren't going anywhere anytime soon. She smeared the heel of her hand across her wet cheek. What did she ever do to deserve a man like Silas in her corner?

"Oh, baby," Silas said as he gathered her on his lap and held her. "It's all going to work out. You'll see."

With a finger under her chin, he raised her face to his and pressed his lips to hers. Tender. A giving without taking. Caring. A sharing without demands. Just the Steady Eddy beat of his heart, and the warmth of his arms around her.

Silas hadn't had time to grab a shirt when he'd followed her to the office. Josephine smelled the dried sweat on his skin, the musk of sex as his bare chest warmed against her cheek.

She wanted a time machine. A quick ride back. Back to twenty minutes ago, when Silas had opened her eyes to what she'd been missing. Opened her eyes to a whole other world of possibilities.

But she couldn't go back in time.

She could only move forward.

She had a lot of thinking to do. As much as she wanted to sink into him and forget all her worries, she couldn't do that.

With reluctance, she stood and helped him to his feet. "I think I'm going for a walk. Clear my head."

"Want company?"

Yes. But this was something Josephine needed to do alone. "Naw. I'm good."

As the sun worked its way through its summer arc, Josephine walked the rodeo grounds looking for direction. She sat at the top of the bleachers looking for perspective, and ended up in the stall where Comet had once stayed, looking to be grounded.

Someone had stripped the stall and dumped a new load of shavings. The sweet scent of pine wafted up, almost masking the undertones of urine where someone hadn't done a good enough job digging out the pee spot.

Where was Comet when she needed him?

Outside the stall, she heard footsteps approach. Chet walked by, his attention on something ahead of him. Then his retreating steps stopped, and a few seconds later, he popped his head around the open stall door. "Hey. You okay?"

"I will be." Eventually.

Chet stepped through the door, his cheeks flushed, and his gaze landed everywhere but on her. What the? Josephine glanced down and realized she was sitting there, sans bra, her body-hugging tank top leaving nothing to the imagination.

She folded her arms over her chest. "Something you needed?"

He looked in her direction, but his focus was on the stall wall somewhere to the left of her head. "I just...I wanted to let you know I didn't say anything."

Josephine sat up straighter. "To who? About what?"

"To your father. About you taking up with—" Chet jerked his head in the general direction of the parking lot and Silas's trailer. "I have to go where Cox tells me to go. But what you do and with who...that's your business. I can't guarantee your father won't hear it from someone else. This business being what it is and all, but if he does, I wanted to let you know it didn't come from me."

"I appreciate that."

Chet nodded, still not able to meet her eye even though her arms covered anything revealing. "And for what it's worth. He's a good man. Foss, I mean. You could do a whole lot worse."

That was the last thing she'd expected to hear coming out of Chet's mouth. He wasn't a man of many words. In the lifetime she'd known him, what he'd just said was probably more than what he'd ever said to her at one time. At least when it hadn't pertained to anything that didn't directly involve the ranch.

"I didn't think you liked him."

"I don't. But that don't make Silas a bad man."

She didn't know what to say to that, so she didn't say anything. Chet stepped out of the stall and stopped. Without looking back, he said, "I know I'm probably the last person you want to hear any advice from, but you should enjoy this time while you can. Your secret is safe with me."

7

Silas knew he was in the right place when he saw Chet
striding down the aisle of stalls where Josephine had kept
Comet during the rodeo. They passed each other with a tight
nod, but no words.

At Comet's stall, Silas stopped and propped a shoulder
against the open sliding door. "Thought I might find you here.
Missing Comet?"

"Mmmm." Josephine nodded. "He's pretty easy to talk to. He
doesn't judge. He doesn't interrupt, and he doesn't mind a few
tears in his mane as long as I bribe him with a flake or two of
alfalfa."

Her smile faltered around the edges, tugging at his guilt. He
should have made her go with Cora. Despite what the doctor
had said, he could have managed on his own. But the truth was,
a small part—make that a not so small part—had been selfish
enough not to argue with her. And now she was hurting. "Have I
told you how much I appreciate what you've sacrificed for me?
You're missing Salinas. Now you miss your horse and..."

"I wanted to do be there for you. You don't have to
thank me."

He may have found her in Comet's old stall, but her tone, her sincerity, confirmed she'd meant what she'd said.

He rammed his hands into his back pocket, felt the material he'd forgotten he's stuffed in there. "Oh, I brought you something."

He pulled her bra out of the back pocket of his jeans, stepped closer and dangled it out in front of her. She snagged her bra out of his hand, and even though they were protected by the walls of the stall, and only a few workers were left at the rodeo grounds, she looked around to make sure no one saw.

"Thank you." She stood and swatted the shavings off her rear. "Turn around."

Silas laughed. "You're kidding me, right? A couple hours ago I had you naked, my—"

"This is different."

He turned his back to her. "How is this different?"

"It just is."

He heard the shuffling of her clothes as she got herself situated. "How long does it take to put on a bra?"

"I'm done, you can turn around."

He turned as she pulled her hair from under her shirt. "I think I liked you better without the bra."

She smiled and thumped his arm with the back of her hand. He caught it and backed her against the wall, the scent of fresh cut wood shavings wafting up. "But do you know what I like more?"

"What's that, cowboy?"

"I like seeing a smile on your face again. Did you get it all figured out?"

"Some of it. A wise man told me something I've taken to heart."

"A wise man, huh?" Silas didn't like that sound of that, especially when he had a pretty good idea who that *wise man* was.

She wrapped her arms around Silas's neck, and he settled his hands on her hips. Then again, if whatever Chet had said put Josephine in his arms, then the wise man was putting a smile on Silas's face as well.

"Care to share?" Silas's thumbs found bare skin, and he traced small circles low on her hip bones.

"I know we agreed to take this, whatever this is between us, one day at a time. I just escaped—I just got out on my own. I'd planned to live a little before I settled down and I'm not looking for a ring or anything, or even to be wearing your belt buckle or—"

"Is there a problem with wearing my belt buckle?" He smiled. Her sentences had started running together again. He loved that talking about the two of them got her flustered.

Because if talking about the two of them got her flustered, then on some level she cared.

"It's just that—"

"Can I say something here?" He hated to interrupt her, but if he didn't say what was on his mind right here, right now, he wasn't sure he'd get it out.

She ducked her head then met his gaze. "Sorry. I'll shut up now."

"I don't want you to shut up, but I want you to hear what I have to say." He turned and brought her with him as he leaned his back against the solid boards of the stall. His head may be feeling better, but he sure as hell wasn't a hundred percent, despite what he wanted Josephine to believe.

She pressed her lips together and ran her fingers over the seam like she was zipping her mouth closed.

"I know you aren't looking for a ring or even a man's boots under your bed. I get that. But hotstuff, when you're ready for those things, I want those boots under your bed to be my size eleven Tony Lamas. I want to be the man who gives you that buckle or that ring. Or whatever the hell it is that will tell the world I'm yours, and you're mine."

She pulled back. The smile vanished from her face. "What are you saying?"

"I'm trying to say, I love you."

The words didn't come as a surprise to him or as some sudden realization of his feelings. From the first time he'd ever seen her, drunk and riding Comet into a crowded bar, he'd been infatuated.

From the first time he'd watched her round that third barrel and gallop toward the alley, he'd been smitten.

From the first time they'd kissed, he'd fallen.

From the first time they'd made love, he'd loved her.

He waited a beat for his words to sink in. His heart hammering his ribs harder and faster than when Bone Crusher had sent him sailing through the air. Beating harder and faster because he knew what she said next could do more permanent damage to him than if that bull had danced the Two-Step on his chest.

Her hands fell from around his neck, and she took another step back. His stomach dropped beneath his boots.

"But we've only been together—"

"A very short time. I get it. But I've had my eye on you for—" Silas scrubbed a hand over his face. "Wait, that sounded creepy. Scratch that." He caught her hands when she tried to pull away. His stomach flattened.

He was blowing this.

He caught a finger under her chin until her eyes met his. "Hear me out?"

She didn't nod, but she took a step closer.

"I know we haven't been together long, but more time won't make my words any truer. I've learned in this business that it's best not to leave things unsaid. So, I'm saying it. I love you."

She started shaking her head as if she wanted to deny it. He held her face in his hands so she could look into his eyes and know his truth. "I love you. And I love the rodeo. But bull riding is a young man's game."

"Young man's game? You're only what? Twenty-six?"

He nodded. "But I won't be twenty-six forever. For me, bull riding is a means to an end. Win my stake. Buy some land. Settle down. Stay in the same town for more than three or four nights in a row. And someday, I want that with you."

"Someday..." The hint of a smile flickered across her face then disappeared as if she were afraid to believe in a future.

"When you're ready. A month. A year. Hell, ten years. I don't care."

"When Cheyenne is over, I'm going home. I realized I can't turn my back on my parents. They need me now. Until then, I want to spend the time I have left with you. But I also don't want to string you along. I can't promise a lifetime. All I can promise you is the next few weeks."

Silas's stomach clawed its way back into his body. Her words didn't mean forever, but they also weren't an outright rejection. He could accept that. After all, he'd been the one to suggest they take things one day at a time and here he was trying to change the rules in the middle of the game.

He should have kept his mouth shut.

Would he be man enough to tell her goodbye when Cheyenne was over and not look back or have regrets?

He hoped he didn't have to find out. "Hotstuff, I'll take what I can get."

He hugged her to him, then took her hand and led her out of the stall, before he did all the things he shouldn't want to do to her in a freshly bedded stall on the outskirts of Calgary.

Josephine had to jog to keep up with his long strides. "Slow down, what's the big rush?"

He had and idea. They left the barn. The sun was setting, and he could already feel the coolness moving in for the night. If they wanted to make California by the weekend, they had to get on the road.

"Salinas," Silas said. "I hear there's a horse there, missing his momma."

"But, the doctor—"

"The doc said to stay put for four days. Which is up tomorrow. A few hours one way or the other isn't going to kill me."

Her smile went as wide as the Canadian Rockies, only more beautiful. He wrapped an arm around her shoulder and steered her toward Chet's truck and camper. He thumped on the back wall by Chet's open door and stuck his head inside. "We're headed to California. We leave in thirty minutes if you wanna caravan."

————

SILAS THUMPED ON THE SIDE OF JOSEPHINE'S TRAILER IN THE rodeo lot in Salinas, poked his head through the open door and said, "You've got five minutes, or Toby and I are leaving for Calamity's to celebrate without you."

Josephine finished tying the ribbon on the end of her braid. "You can't leave without me, it's my celebration."

"Five minutes. We'll swing by and pick you up." Silas jogged back toward his truck and camper before she could protest.

She plucked her best straw hat from the hanger above the door and stomped her feet into her bar boots—the turquoise ones with the two-inch heels that matched her one and only western skirt. The skirt hit her mid-thigh and made her a little self-conscious, but somehow, she'd let Cora talk her into buying it. It wasn't like she was trying to catch a man.

In the few days since they'd left Calgary, Silas hadn't told her again that he loved her. He wasn't the kind of man who was mushy or sappy or showered women with gifts. Instead, he showed his love in the little things he did for her every day. Like mucking out Comet's stall and hauling heavy water buckets and making sure she had enough hay and waiting in the alley for her after her run.

More importantly, he hadn't pressured her into saying she loved him back.

Since he wasn't the type to play head games, he'd just laid his heart at her feet. She admired his confidence as well as his vulnerability as he waited for her to decide if she would stomp his heart into the ground and kick it aside, or pick it up and keep it forever.

As Toby pulled up, the engine in his old truck coughing more than chugging, Silas slid out the passenger side of the single cab, and she scooted to the middle of the bench seat, her feet straddling the hump.

"Hey, Toby."

"Hey, beautiful."

Silas growled. Toby grinned and let out a loud whoop through the open window as he tromped on the accelerator. The engine wheezed, then backfired, then lurched forward, gaining momentum. Cora and that bulldogger—Josh?—came running out of the rodeo office and intercepted them.

"Can we catch a ride?" Cora leaned through Toby's window, giving Silas's friend an appraising once-over as if she were already picking out her next victim, or conquest, or whatever the heck you could call the men in Cora's life these days.

Toby gestured toward the bed of his truck with his thumb. Cora and her guy jumped into the tail bed. Toby had to stop two more times and pick up more riders before he'd made it out of the parking lot. The added weight made the rear springs sag, and the overloaded truck's nose point in the air like a plane ready for takeoff.

Luckily, Calamity's was only one turn and two backfires away from the rodeo grounds. Toby parked, and the rider's in the back spilled out. A few handed over a dollar or two for the ride. The rest scattered, except for Cora and Josh who followed Josephine, Silas, and Toby into the bar and grill.

That late at night, Calamities was like any other bar close to a rodeo on a Saturday night—crowded, loud. The rowdy weekend cowboys already full of whiskey and testosterone, and one wrong look or slung insult away from a fight.

Most of the pros nursed their beers or had hit the sack early, catching up on sleep for their events the next day.

On their way to an empty booth, one of the weekend boys spotted Toby's long black braid, and the single bear claw strung around his neck from a piece of leather. The idiot placed two fingers behind his head like feathers and made an obnoxious *wah, wah, wah, wah, wah, wah, wah* sound as he patted his hand over his mouth like a five-year-old playing cowboys and Indians.

Dropping Josephine's hand, Silas stalked toward the drunk and his minions who belly laughed like they'd never seen anything so damn funny. Toby caught Silas by the shoulder, a brisk, "Leave 'em," coming out of his mouth.

Silas shook off Toby's hand but allowed his friend to steer him back toward the booth.

Josephine and Cora slid in on opposite sides of the table. Silas sat next to her, and Josh slid in next to Cora. Toby hijacked a chair and sat at the end of the table.

"I don't know how you put up with that shit," Silas said. "Just let me at them. Five minutes. Hell, I'm so pissed I don't even need that long. I can do plenty of damage in two. I've seen Josh's right hook. We could get it done in one."

"It's not worth it. Trust me." Toby leaned back in his chair, his shoulders relaxed but a muscle twitched by his right eye.

The waitress came by and left with their food and drink orders. A stray *wah, wah, wah,* drifted to them over the laughter and the shouts and the jukebox.

Silas glanced over his shoulder, his muscles tight as the idiot did his version of a native dance between the tables.

Toby socked Silas in the arm. "Stop. We're here to celebrate Josephine, not mop the floor with a couple of assho_es."

The waitress returned with a pitcher of beer and five frozen mugs. Toby poured, and when everyone had a glass, they clacked them together.

"To Josephine," Silas said.

"To Josephine," the rest of them echoed.

"Y'all are going to curse me." Josephine had only been half kidding.

Cora swallowed and wiped the foam from her upper lip. "All you have to do is finish near the top tomorrow night and next week and Cheyenne is yours for the taking."

"There's still a lot that can go wrong. Comet could come up lame, or we could crash into the third can or—"

"Hush." Silas put his arm around her shoulder and kissed the side of her head. "Nothing is going to go wrong."

He took a sip of his beer and said to the rest of the group, "Josephine is convinced the circuit is plagued with bad luck or juju or whatever you want to call it. I keep trying to convince her that—"

Josh shook a finger at Josephine as if to say she might have a point. "A bulldogger friend of mine dislocated his shoulder a week back when a steer flipped him."

"Johnny Freeman's transmission blew out last month, and he was stuck on the side of the road all night long," Toby added.

Cora swallowed a mouthful of beer. "And that redhead on the flag team caught her boyfriend cheating—"

"That asshole always cheats," Silas said. "That's not bad juju, that's bad judgment."

Everyone nodded their heads in agreement. "Maybe." Cora topped off Josh's beer. "But that roper guy, Jester was it? He threw his back out. Sharp pains, he said, like someone was jabbing pins in a voodoo doll and—"

"Stop. All of you." Silas clacked the bottom of his mug on the table. "The circuit isn't cursed. There's no bad juju, and no one is running around with a pocket full of pins and a voodoo doll."

The waitress brought their food, and they all dug into their burgers and fries.

"Besides," Silas said around a bite of beef, "Toby made eight tonight on Tupelo. Only one other person has stayed on that bull since the spring."

Josh clacked his mug against Toby's. "And here I thought you were skipping this rodeo."

"Got tossed in the first go around in Rock Springs. But I hadn't canceled this one, so I busted my ass and got here just in time to ride."

Starved, Josephine scooped up some ketchup with her french fries tuning out some of the conversation. Despite what Silas had said about the circuit not being cursed, she couldn't shake that weight in the bottom of her belly like someone had tossed in an old rusty horseshoe and it was just sitting there festering.

"...and you'll never guess which bull I drew for tomorrow night." Toby had his burger to his mouth, and he tore off a hunk, tucking the bite into his cheek. "Thrasher."

That horseshoe flopped in Josephine's belly. Josh laughed. Silas stilled. Cora said, "Who's Thrasher?"

Silas's hand tightened on Josephine's thigh. He leaned toward Toby and said, "You don't have to ride him."

The crowd had thinned out, and no one had bothered

dumping any more quarters in the jukebox, so Josephine didn't have any problem hearing Silas's soft-spoken words.

"Come on, buddy." Toby washed his burger down with some beer. "I thought you didn't believe in all that bad juju bullshit."

"I don't. It's just—"

"*Hello.*" Cora waved her arms around until she had everyone's attention. She wasn't a woman who liked to be ignored. "Who is this Thrasher?"

"A bad bull." Josephine looked at Silas for confirmation. "What's the score now? Thrasher three hundred. Bull riders zero?"

"Awh, he ain't that bad." Toby threw in a laugh, but it kinda fell flat.

"Nobody's ever gone the eight seconds on him," Josephine said. "That rodeo announcer said some consider him unrideable."

Silas glanced at her, a smile on his face somewhere between surprise and pride. What had he expected? When you took a bull rider to your bed, you tended to take an interest in the animals who wanted to stomp him into the ground.

"Darling," Toby said, "they're all unrideable until someone does."

Josephine peeled Silas's hand off her thigh and linked her fingers with his before she lost all circulation to the lower part of her leg.

Silas pushed a pickle around his plate. "You can pull. You don't have to ride him."

"If I want to get to Cheyenne I do."

"Yeah, but—"

Toby clapped a hand on Silas's back. His eyes bright and his used-car-salesman smile wide as if that would help convince Silas everything was good. "Relax, buddy. I've got a good feeling about tomorrow."

8

———

On his way to the chutes, Silas passed Rowdy Boyd heading the other way, all decked out in his gaudy rodeo clown garb, his smile painted on thick and his red nose stuck in place.

He shouldered past Silas without glancing up, his steps quick with a don't-screw-with-me-vibe radiating outward like a nuclear cloud.

Silas reversed and came up behind the clown. "Hey, Boyd."

Rowdy stopped, but he didn't turn around.

"You okay?"

"I-I'm f-fine."

Silas put his hand on Rowdy's shoulder. "Look, if Monte's been riding your ass—"

"M-Monte's not the problem."

"Then what is?"

Rowdy turned around. Slow. One step then another and another until they faced each other. He kicked at an old dried-up cow patty with the tip of his shoes, then met Silas's gaze. "It's g-good to see you out of the h-h-hospital and doing well. I-I hate to see you guys get h-hurt."

If Rowdy didn't want to talk about what was bothering him,

Silas had to respect that. "Thanks, man. We appreciate what you do for us. Except Monte, but he's an asshole, so don't worry about him."

"Yeah. I h-hear ya. Karma's a b-bitch, right?" Rowdy had a smile on his face and this time it wasn't just the makeup kind.

Rowdy clapped Silas on the shoulder. "S-see you around."

The announcer came on the PA and Silas hurried over to where Thrasher had been loaded into the number one chute. He caught up with Toby before his friend could climb up the rails.

Toby grinned, all white teeth and adrenaline-fueled anticipation. "Hey buddy, decided to watch me from the cheap seats?"

"It's not too late to back out."

"You're kidding me, right? Your brains are scrambled if you think I'm going to—"

"It's not worth the risk, Tobe."

"You know, you suck at this best friend thing. You're the one who's supposed to have my back. You're the one who's supposed to be cheering me on."

"Bail. You've got a good draw next week and—"

"Fuck that. Unlike you, I have to ride this weekend. I've done the math. I can't get to Cheyenne without at least finishing in the money this weekend and next."

"There's always next year."

"Navarro," Terry Lewis called out to Toby from the chutes. "Kiss your boyfriend goodbye and get your *injun* ass over here."

Thrasher rammed his head at the end of the chute and kicked at the rails behind him. The bull kicked again, and the chute clanked and shuttered.

"I don't want to wait. If we both finish high in the money in Cheyenne, there won't have to be a next year. Have a little faith."

"*Navarro!*"

"Hold your horses," Toby hollered back. Toby turned his

attention back to Silas. His eyes sharp, the bravado putting an extra spark in his eyes. "Bet on me, buddy. I'm liking my chances."

"Yeah." Silas painted on a smile. They both pretended it was real. "Break a leg."

Toby barked out a laugh and climbed up the rails and straddled the chute. Thrasher reared, his front hooves beating against the rails. He caught a fetlock over the top. The bull pissed and shit and yanked before getting his leg free and slamming down on all fours. Thrasher's lungs bellowed, his foot pawed, his tail swished.

Toby stood on top of the rails and waved his hat to the crowd. The stands erupted. Cheers and foot stomping drowned out the announcer. They started chanting *To-by, To-by, To-by.* Each syllable thumping against Silas's eardrums in a deafening two-part rhythm.

Silas scrambled on top of one of the empty chutes as Toby adjusted his bullrope. The chants died back, and the crowd fell quiet, the anticipation so thick in the air that Silas couldn't quite catch his breath. He felt a hand low on his back, and he looked down to see Josephine behind him.

He gave her a hand up the rails and she sat on top, hooking the heels of her boots on the rail below her. She grabbed his hand.

"Shouldn't you be getting Comet cooled down?" He had to talk louder than normal, but he didn't have to shout.

"One of the stable guys owes me a favor." She bobbed her chin in Toby's direction. "Is he good enough?"

"One of the best."

"It'll be all right then." By the way she squeezed his hand, Silas wasn't convinced she believed her own words.

He kissed the back of her hand and held it to his chest. "Sure, it will."

Silas locked his gaze on the number one chute. Toby had wrapped his hand with the tail of his rope, slid up Thrasher's back, and straddled the rope. He snugged his hat down to his ears and gave the gateman a quick nod.

The chute opened, and Thrasher spun out of the gate. Dirt clods flew, pelting Silas and Josephine. She swiped a hand across her forehead leaving a red smear.

In the arena, Toby and Thrasher battled. Toby dug in his spurs as Thrasher bucked and spun and tossed Toby around like a wet towel caught on the spin cycle.

Four more seconds.

Thrasher twisted then stuck his head between his knees and kicked his heels into the air, catching Toby off balance.

Three seconds.

Toby re-centered, landing with a ground shaking thud that made Silas's kidneys cry out in sympathy. Toby would be lucky not to be pissing blood for the next week.

Two seconds.

"Go, Toby!" Josephine stood on one of the rails, her hands on Silas's shoulders for balance, her voice hoarse as she cheered on his friend. Then her nails dug into his shoulder like talons as Toby's left leg came off the bull's side and swung back behind his center of gravity.

"No, no, no, no," Silas yelled. He could see it coming, knew what was going to happen before it even happened. He was reaching for the top rail to swing his legs over when Toby's momentum threw him forward as Thrasher's head slammed up, catching Toby in the forehead.

Toby's body went limp.

His right hand caught in the rigging.

The bullfighters ran in as the buzzer sounded. Toby's dead weight flopping around on Thrashers back. Rowdy bounced in front of the bull, trying to distract him as one of the other clowns ran in to grab the bullrope to free Toby. The crowd went silent, and Sila's ears rang in the aftermath. The smell of shit, piss, sausages, and popcorn filled his nostrils.

Thrasher swung his massive head at Rowdy, hooking Toby beneath the arm with one of his horns, slinging Toby's body clear.

Silas didn't wait for the bull to be corralled. He jumped down into the arena and sprinted to his friend, stumbling in the thick dirt. He scrambled back to his feet.

"Watch out!" One of the clowns yelled as he ran by, but Silas wasn't worried about the bull. He was worried about his friend.

Silas slid to his knees by Toby's head. There was a gash on Toby's forehead and blood trickled down into his hair. He held Toby's head steady. They must have run the bull out of the arena because the paramedics ran in with their gear and a backboard.

One of the paramedics cut the front of Toby's shirt open. Was Toby even breathing? From beneath Toby's left arm, a wound bubbled with blood and air.

Toby groaned, his hand coming to his face, but with his hand still caught in the bullrope, he only managed to slap himself with it.

"Hold still, Tobe. I'm here, man. Let them check you out."

Silas locked Toby's head between his knees and freed his friend's hand from the rigging. Something niggled in the back of Silas's head. More of a polite tap on the shoulder than a slap in the face. But he couldn't think about that now.

His thoughts, his focus, was on Toby.

Someone tugged on Silas's arm. "You gotta let him go. Silas...*Silas.*"

———

"SILAS? ARE YOU BACK HERE? *SILAS*?" JOSEPHINE AIMED HER

flashlight under the bleachers near the chutes, where many of the bull riders had staged their gear before their rides. She'd already checked Toby's trailer for Silas, but it had a quiet, almost abandoned feeling to it.

Toby was alive and out of surgery, but with him being on a ventilator, the doctors didn't have any plans to try and wake him for a day or so at the earliest. The doctors had ordered Silas back to the rodeo grounds to get some rest. But Silas had walked off as soon as they'd pulled back into camp. That had been hours ago.

Now the sun would be up soon. Where was he? Had he caught a ride back to the hospital and didn't tell her? Josephine couldn't shake the sickeningly sweet taste that kept climbing up the back of her throat, like she needed to vomit, but her stomach was too empty, too twisted, to accomplish anything more than make spit pool in her mouth.

Off to her left she heard a noise like boots scuffing on gravel and swung the beam of her flashlight around. "There you are."

She picked her way through the maze of crisscrossed supports and eased down beside him, resting her back against the pillar. "You want to talk about it?"

"No." One word. Steady. Unequivocal. He didn't move. His head rested against the pillar, his hat over his eyes, his legs crossed at the ankles, a bullrope in his hands.

"Congrats on your ride." His hands rubbed on a section of the rope just past a sticky section of rosin.

She didn't want to talk about her ride. But at this point she'd talk about anything, even her dad, if it kept Silas talking.

"We did well enough to qualify for the finals this weekend." With a hundredth of a second to spare.

"You should get some sleep. Comet deserves to have a well-rested rider for the finals tomorrow."

Off to the east, past the locked-up concession stands and the empty public parking lot and the battered chain link, the inky black night had turned a shade lighter. "Make that today."

Silas tipped up his hat far enough that he could see the pinks blossoming on the horizon. He looked at her then, the pain in his eyes was a raw, palpable beast he was either too tired, or too emotionally battered to muzzle and leash. "All the more reason you should get some sack time."

"Come with me."

He gave the slightest shake of his head, so she settled against him. He put his arm around her and laid her head against his chest. She silently vowed to stay awake with him even as her eyes started to cross. The deep-seated fatigue from the stress of the past week or so was taking its toll and her runs were suffering.

But as important as it was to her to make it to Cheyenne, knowing that she had to go home after, no matter how well she did, stole some of her drive. Now with Toby in the hospital...

Snakebit, bad juju, bad luck, cards stacked against them, whatever the heck was going on this circuit, Josephine wanted it to stop.

Silas stiffened beside her and he sucked in a *holy-shit* type breath.

Her eyes flew open and she struggled to sit up. "What is it?"

He held up the end of Toby's bullrope, the end jagged and frayed.

"I don't understand."

"Someone cut this rope."

———

"WHAT DO YOU MEAN SOMEONE CUT THE ROPE?" JOSEPHINE grabbed the end of the rope and held it up to the rising sun. "It looks like it split. The strands are frayed and—"

"Look close. Right there." Silas pointed to the flat side of the rope, then spun it a hundred and eighty degrees in her hand. "And here. Like someone ran a knife along both sides."

"But Toby was knocked out by the bull. The bullfighters got him free."

Silas replayed Toby's ride in his head, his stomach taking a nose dive as the bull's hard head hammered Toby's. None of that had anything to do with a split rope. Once Toby had been knocked out, one of the clowns had made a grab for the rope around Toby's lifeless hand, but had come up short when Thrasher spun. *That's* when Toby had been thrown clear.

That mental tap on his shoulder he'd felt when he'd released Toby's hand from the rigging reached up and slapped him in the face. "You were right."

"I was? About what?"

"About the bad juju. Well, maybe not about the bad juju, but about something not being right. I think someone's sabotaging the bull rides." He stumbled to his feet, his stiff muscles bitching and complaining and generally giving him shit, but he ignored all that. "Come on."

She took the hand he offered, and he helped her up. "Where we going?"

"To check my rope from last weekend." Nervous energy drove him back toward his rig at a ground eating pace.

Josephine jogged beside him to keep up. "Why would someone want to sabotage the bull rides? Who would benefit?"

"I don't know. Someone who has something to gain by keeping the top riders out of the running in Cheyenne. Someone who may not have a shot at a buckle otherwise. Or someone with a lot of money on the wrong guy."

At his truck, Silas threw open the back door of his camper and tossed his rigging bag on the ground. He hadn't even looked in it since his concussion. He opened it wide and dumped the contents onto the gravel parking lot. Tossing aside a bunch of miscellaneous trash and other crap that had accumulated over a season on the circuit, he carefully inspected his backup bullrope and found nothing wrong.

Josephine reached over and nabbed the rope he'd used, the bells clanking and clattering. "Uh, oh."

He didn't like the sound of that. He stopped what he was doing and took the end of the rope from her. Knife marks. Just like Toby's.

"This is beyond ride fixing," Josephine said. "Toby could have been killed. *You* could have been killed."

He thought back to his ride, back to who could get ahead in the earnings with him and Toby out of the picture and Monte Shaw popped into his head. With Silas out for a weekend and Toby out for God only knew how long, Monte had moved up in the standings. He wasn't in the top ten earnings yet, but depending on how this and next weekend went, he could be.

The blood in Silas's veins went cold then hot. "That son of a bitch."

"Who?" Josephine started shoving all his gear back into his bag.

"Monte."

"What? You don't seriously believe Monte is behind this do you? He's an ass, but I don't see him cutting people's ropes and waiting on the sidelines for something bad to happen. Besides, if you wanted to rig a ride, certainly there's a better way. Who's to say the rope is going to snap when you want it to? And wanting to win is a long way from attempted murder."

They heard laughter coming from a few rigs over. A little too obnoxious. A little too much bravado. A woman giggled. High pitched. Calculating. He glanced at Josephine. How the hell did he get so lucky to land the finest woman on the circuit?

"Speak of the devil," Josephine said with a head toss in the direction of the laughter.

Silas balled up his rope. "Wait here."

Josephine put a staying hand on his arm. "Where you going?"

"To see a man about a rope."

Josephine fell into step beside him. He stopped. "Stay."

She raised a brow, her gaze hard, but held a hint of humor. "If you think I'm a dog you can—"

"What are you going to do, fight my fights for me?"

"If I have to." Her chin came up a couple notches. "You still aren't a hundred percent. You're still having headaches and you can't make it through the afternoon without needing to rest. No way are you ready for a fight."

Damn. All she needed was a red and blue bodysuit with a giant W across her chest. Despite how bone weary he was, all he wanted to do was take her back to his camper, back to his bed, and put all her piss and vinegar to good use.

Instead, he wrapped an arm around her shoulder and pressed a kiss to the side of her head. "Come on, hotstuff."

Her eyes lit as if he'd said he'd bought her a brand-new barrel saddle. She was easy to please. One of the many things he was learning to love about her.

They came around the corner of a faded red two-horse bumper pull. Monte had a young local girl backed against his rig, his hands on her ass and his tongue down her throat. Josephine drew up short. "Maybe we should come back later," she whispered.

Oh hell no. Silas's blood bubbled as it climbed to a soft, rolling boil. "Monte, I need a word."

Monte pulled back from the girl but didn't bother to turn their way. This was probably the most action Monte had seen in a while. The women on the circuit had learned their lesson the hard way, and pretty much treated him like a feral dog. Nice enough to pat, but too dirty to take home.

"Go away," Monte said.

The girl skittered away with the briefest look back. Monte fastened the top button of his jeans and buckled his belt. "What the hell do you want?"

Silas tossed the bullrope and it hit Monte square in the chest. "You so desperate to win that you gotta cheat to get to the top?"

Monte caught the rope before it tumbled to the ground. "I ain't no cheat."

"You're saying you had nothing to do with cutting my rope? Or Toby's?"

"Cuttin your—" Monte leveled his eyes on Silas. "What the hell kind of drugs did that ER doc give you? I didn't cut yours or anybody else's rope. I don't need to cheat to win."

Monte tossed the rope back at Silas, but Silas let it fall to the ground. He closed the gap between him and Monte. "You were in my trailer right before my ride. You had plenty—"

"Wait." Josephine wedged herself between the two of them and pushed them apart. She turned on Monte. "You were in his trailer? Before his ride?

Monte's eyes went dark and his hands fisted at his sides. Silas placed his hands on her shoulders, prepared to yank her out of the way if a fist went flying. Monte caught the movement, his lip twitched up into a sneer, but his hand relaxed. Silas may not be a hundred percent, but if that asshole messed up one hair on Josephine's head, it would take the sheriff and all his deputies to pull him off Monte's bloody body.

"I was returning some money I owed. Not that I need to justify my actions to a bi—"

"You don't want to finish that sentence." He didn't yell. The quiet confidence with which he said those words was enough of a warning that Monte shut his trap. Though really, Silas would kill for an excuse to land another fat one on the side of Monte's face.

"You don't have to justify it to me." All smoldering fire and leashed indignation. God, she was beautiful when she was riled. She poked a finger in Monte's sternum hard enough to make him wince.

Looked like Silas had been protecting the wrong person. If the pulse thumping at the base of her throat and the tautness in her shoulders was any indication, Monte was one stupid response away from Silas having to haul her off Monte's battered body, kicking and screaming.

Silas almost smiled. No other woman had ever made him so hard so fast. He readjusted himself.

"But I'm going to make sure you have to justify it to the rodeo commission, and the sheriff," Josephine said.

She turned on her heels and had taken a few steps towards the rodeo office when she turned back to Silas and said, "You coming?"

"Right behind you."

"You're not much of a man if your woman has to fight your battles for you."

Despite the taunt, Silas smiled. *Your woman.* He liked the sound of that. Liked that others saw that too, even if Josephine refused to admit it herself. Silas bent down and picked up his rope. "Watch yourself, Monte. You go anywhere near anything that doesn't belong to you, and the sheriff will be the least of your worries."

Monte tucked his thumbs in the front pockets of his jeans but managed to keep his big mouth closed.

Josephine was already out of sight. He'd probably have to peel her off the rodeo chairman too if the man didn't take their claims seriously. He wouldn't want to miss that. Silas turned to follow.

"How is he?" Monte asked.

Silas stopped, but didn't turn around.

"Navarro," Monte said. "I heard he's in a coma."

There had been something in Monte's voice that sounded a whole lot like genuine concern. Silas turned around.

"I know I can be an asshole sometimes, and I have no fucking idea what Josephine sees in a prick like you, but everybody likes Navarro. He was a good man."

Was. The word smacked Silas as if Muhammad Ali had hauled off and sucker punched him in the gut. Acid rolled up the back of Silas's his esophagus scorching the back of his throat. "Is." The word came out charred and brittle. Silas cleared his throat. "Toby *is* a good man."

Silas wasn't sure what Monte was trying to say. Was it some sort of apology for hurting a fellow competitor? For leaving a good man in a coma? Or was Monte's concern real?

9

"WHAT DO YOU MEAN THERE'S NOTHING YOU CAN DO?" JOSEPHINE stared at the Monterey county sheriff, unable to process his words.

Sheriff Baldwin was an older man with more hair in his ears than on the top of his head and a belly that strained the limits of the buttons holding his shirt together. "Like I said, I'll have one of my deputies ask around, see if anyone saw someone messing with Mr. Navarro's rigging bag, but the area behind the chutes isn't secure. Anyone could have slipped back there unnoticed."

"What about Monte? And Silas's rope? Silas caught Monte coming out of his camper that same day his rope was cut."

The sheriff leaned a shoulder against the wall of the rodeo office, resting his forearms on his pistol and nightstick. "And Mr. Shaw denies any wrongdoing. It's Mr. Foss's word against Mr. Shaw's."

"What about fingerprints?"

The sheriff barked out a laugh, full of condescension. "Ma'am," he said, though in her head she heard *look here little Missy.* "No need getting all hysterical."

"*Hysterical?*" And yeah, that squeak in her voice did come

out a tad unbalanced. But they were talking about men's lives at stake here. Didn't that deserve a little emotion? A little passion?

She took a step toward the sheriff, not exactly sure what she'd had in mind, but Silas gripped a gentling hand around her elbow. How could he be so calm? She spun on him. "How can you be so calm? This is your life, your friends' lives."

"And one way or the other we'll get to the bottom of this." Silas's words came out even and reasonable, but she saw the strain around his eyes, and the fight in the set of his jaw and the squaring of his shoulders.

The sheriff must have seen it too because he said, "Now son, don't you be getting any cockamamie ideas in that noggin of yours."

Silas didn't spare the sheriff a glance and Josephine knew there was nothing the sheriff could say to dissuade Silas from doing his own poking around. There was too much at stake to leave it in the hands of a sheriff who knew that the rodeo would be out of his jurisdiction in a little less than twenty-four hours. She could almost see the man mentally counting down the minutes until this trouble, whatever the hell it was, was someone else's.

Silas leveled his gaze on Maynard Rowe, the man responsible for putting on many of the rodeos they'd entered on the road to Cheyenne. "I'm not surprised the sheriff doesn't give two damns—"

"Hey there, son—"

Silas talked over the sheriff as if he hadn't been interrupted. "But this circuit is your livelihood. The word gets out you aren't doing everything in your power to get to the bottom of this, you can bet your ass everyone will be riding Silver's rodeos next year."

Maynard was an old coot with an unlit cigar mashed in the corner of his mouth that always made his vowels sound round and his consonants land soft. Maynard's eyes narrowed, and he pulled his cigar out of his mouth long enough to spit something on the floor as if the mention of his rival rodeo promoter soured on his tongue. "You threatening me, boy?"

"It's not a threat. It's not even a promise. It just is."

"Now, son—"

Silas shut the sheriff up with a look Josephine imagined he'd had right before he'd decked Monte a couple weeks ago. "Don't you have a job that needs doing, Sheriff?"

Slowly, the sheriff stood to his full height. Silas still had a good five inches on him, and while Silas had never seemed the type to lord his height over another man, Josephine recognized that light in Silas's eyes. He was enjoying the hell out of the fact that the sheriff had to tilt his head back to look him in the eye.

The sheriff held Silas's gaze long enough to let Silas know that Silas hadn't chased him off, or some macho-man bull crap like that. To Maynard, the sheriff said, "Rowe, I'll be getting in touch."

The sheriff left, and Silas stared at Maynard across the battered desk where Maynard worried the end of his cigar the way a feral dog might gnaw a bone. "You need to call off the bull riding tonight. It's not safe."

"Safe? *Safe?*" Maynard's chuckle was thick with phlem. "You think people come to the rodeo for the barrel racing? No. They watch the barrel racing, but come for the bull riding. I'm not pulling the money maker. No one forces you idiots to ride."

Silas planted his palms on the narrow desk. Maynard had to lean back in the chair to get Silas out of his face. "No one forces us to ride, but this sport is dangerous enough without someone besides the bull trying to kill us."

"I'll block off the area behind the chutes, post some men. But I'm not canceling the bull ride, and if you cause me any trouble,

I'll find a way to make the Pro Bull Riding association sanction your ass. You'd be lucky to catch-ride sheep at a 4-H carnival."

"Now who's tossing around the threats?"

Maynard stuffed his mouth with the cigar again. "No, boy. *That* is a promise."

———

"YOU OKAY?" JOSEPHINE'S VOICE DRIFTED TO SILAS IN THE NEAR darkness of his camper. The perimeter of the parking lot was edged with vapor lamps and the yellow light filtered in around the edge of the blinds.

"I'm fine," he said, but the way the words came out, *fine* was a hard days ride from where he was. He was exhausted but couldn't sleep. Seeing Toby earlier that night, still in a medically induced coma, hadn't made him feel any better. Toby's mother blaming Silas for Toby's injuries hadn't helped. Not that Mrs. Navarro would ever come right out and say it, but he'd seen it in her rheumy eyes, as if she'd thought it was him that should have been lying in that bed instead of her son.

It wouldn't do to tell her that he'd tried to talk Toby out of the ride. She wouldn't want to hear it. Besides, in a corner of his mind, he knew he held part of the blame. If it hadn't been for him, Toby would still be on the reservation, safe, but trapped in a way of life he couldn't escape. Silas had convinced him that bull riding was his way out. He'd been right.

But that only made Silas feel worse.

"Yeah. Sure you're fine. Your mattress probably has permanent damage the way you've been flopping around," Josephene said.

"Sorry." Silas sat up and threw his legs over the side of the bed, too restless to sleep, and too exhausted to get up.

The mattress dipped, and Josephine came up behind him,

draping her arms over his shoulders, her bare breasts soft against his back.

She pressed a kiss to the side of his neck, her breath warm. He could stay like that forever, wrapped up in her, in them, shutting out the rest of the world. But he had an obligation to keep his friends and fellow riders safe.

"Come back to bed." Her words held a tantalizing promise that he couldn't ignore.

He reached behind him, capturing the back of her neck with his hand and held her close. "And if I do? What will I get?" He knew the answer, but it turned him on to hear it coming from her lips.

"Me."

His needs turned dark and all he wanted to do was take whatever she'd give him.

Just for a moment, he wanted to forget about his friend, wanted to forget about his worries, wanted to forget there was some sick bastard out there who wanted to hurt him and his friends.

Just for a moment, all he wanted was his Josephine.

Hard and hot and fast and... "Careful what you wish for, hotstuff."

He turned his head to see her reaction. She didn't frown at the darkness in his voice. She smiled. Sad. Knowing. The shine in her eyes saying whatever he dished out, she would gladly take.

He stood and turned to face her. "Lie back."

She did as he asked, her breasts jiggling in a way that made him want to lick his way up her belly and burrow his face between them.

He shucked his briefs and made her panties disappear even faster. His breath caught as he took in the sight of her. Silas ran the tips of his fingers over the muscular curve of her calves used to direct her horse, over her firm thighs that kept her tight in the saddle, up to her flat belly that kept her balanced in the tight turns.

Her hands skimmed over his shoulders, the tiny callouses on her palms raising the hair on his arms and sending sensations through his body that made him think of tangled sheets, sweaty nights, and long-lasting orgasms.

"Hurry." Her soft brown eyes darkened, not so innocent anymore, as she reached for him.

He dodged her hand. She pouted. It was adorable, and he wanted to take that bottom lip and nip and suck on it. Grasping her ankles, he tugged her ass to the edge of the bed and wrapped her legs around his waist, his cock brushing over the top of her mound. She moaned, arching up, her body seeking the pressure and her release. He blocked her hand again and caught the errant wrist, trapping her arm low across her belly.

"Hotstuff, there is nothing that excites me more than having your hands on me, but if you touch me right now, the fat lady's not only going to sing, she's going to shatter the crystal."

Josephine got a mischievous look on her face that promised wicked pleasure. Sweat popped out on his forehead as he struggled to maintain control. Silas eased forward, the bead of hot pre-cum slicking her folds and the ridge of his penis teasing her nub. He recognized the glint in her eye a micro-second too late. With her free hand, she reached across and curled her fingers around him, her grip firm, her strokes enticingly long and dangerously slow.

In one quick motion, she tipped her pelvis up and dug her heels into his ass, driving him so deep, so fast, their breaths hissed in at the same time. Her head lolled to the side, a ball busting 'O' shape to her lips. If he weren't already in a tight, warm, space, he wouldn't have been able to sleep until those magnificent, plump lips slid down his shaft.

With a hand under her ass, he lifted her hips and stuffed a pillow beneath her, loving the angle, the depth, the tension. The muscles in her belly quivered beneath his hand as he stroked in and out. The tingling of his impending orgasm tightened his balls. He pulled out until only the tip remained inside her, ready to plunge into to her again, to take her hard and fast. She bucked up against him taking him impossibly deep. Every inch of her hot, slick, encompassing. She felt—

He stilled. His hands clasping her thighs, his fingertips digging into her soft flesh.

Her eyes shot open, and she raised her head. Her hips rising and falling, determined to keep the slow, sensuous rhythm. "Don't you dare sto—"

"I forgot the condom."

No wonder she felt so amazing.

But as soon as he thought it, he knew the way she felt had more to do with how she'd wormed her way under his skin than the fact there was no barrier between them.

She stilled, and he waited for the realization of what he'd said to sink in, waited for her to scramble away. To get angry. To tell him what an idiot he was.

To regret it.

Instead, she met his gaze, her internal muscles milking him. Her eyes drifted closed, the pink tip of her tongue trailing over her bottom lip. He caught her hips with his hands and stilled her motion before he completely lost his shit and didn't give a rat's ass that they had no protection.

It didn't matter that she was on birth control. Nothing was a hundred percent, and she'd made it clear she had no intention of chasing kids and cans at the same time. Besides, an unplanned pregnancy wasn't the only concern.

Josephine writhed beneath him, a low whine of complaint drifted between her parted lips. And because he couldn't help himself, he slid his hand over her mound, scrunching his fingers through her soft, tight curls. He pressed down with gentle pressure to still her, but she surged against his open palm.

He could have pulled out, *should* have pulled out. But he didn't. "Did you hear what I said?" If she left it up to him, he'd stay like that forever. Slick. Slippery. Sheathed.

"I heard you."

His thumb slid down one incredible inch, circling her clit and enticing a dick hardening moan from her lips. If he was trying to stop her, he was doing a piss poor job of it. "Stop. We should stop." Even as he said it, the curve of his lips matched hers, his words lacking complete conviction. Or any form of conviction at all.

She stopped, propping herself on her elbows and looked him up and down. That tingle in his balls got worse instead of better, and he rubbed his thumb into her folds.

"Do—" Her head drifted back. "Damn that feels so good. You aren't making this easy." She raised her head. "Do you want to stop?" There was no teasing in her tone, as her internal muscles quivered and quaked.

He gritted his teeth. This was important. This was a potentially life-altering decision. One that had no business being made while their hormones revved like jet engines, and their heart beats drowned out all rational thought.

"No," he said. The word came out rough. Strangled. As if the word had been raked over shattered glass. He swallowed, but very little saliva remained in his mouth, and his throat clicked with the dry motion. "But I don't want to make any mistakes with you. You're too important. *We're* too important."

Her fingers stroked the hair on the back of his hand that still rested at the apex of her thighs. "I've never had sex without a condom. You?"

"Never."

"And you said you loved me."

He smiled. Liking the way her eyes lost focus when she said those words, like she was picturing them and maybe their future. Together. "I did. I do."

"I don't have plans to make love with anyone else. Do you?" One of her delicate brows arched.

Make love. Not have sex. He took a fraction of a moment to internalize the sentiment, knowing there was only one right answer to this question. One he didn't hesitate when answering. "Not on your life."

"I love the feel of you. Just you. I don't want to stop. If there are any consequences, then we'll deal with them together. Okay?"

Which kind of implied that they would still be together, even though she'd given their relationship an expiration date. Two weeks, fourteen days, three hundred plus hours. Give or take.

But who was counting?

She laid down again, locking her ankles behind his ass and driving him deep. He sucked in a breath and almost didn't hear her over the *squish-whoosh* of the blood behind his eardrums when she said, "And Silas, one more thing...I want you to make me scream."

She didn't have to repeat herself.

Widening his stance, he latched onto her hips as he plundered and plunged. Her breaths came in short, staccato bursts, her breasts bouncing, her eyes squeezed shut against the relentless pounding. She reached her arms over her head, her palms braced against the wall of the camper. Giving him everything she got. Everything she was.

He hadn't thought she'd held back the other times they'd made love, but as she shattered around him, as she screamed his name, as he shot his seed deep into her womb, as her eyes fluttered open and met his gaze, he felt her love.

She didn't have to say it. Her body said it for her.

He collapsed on top of her. Their bodies sticking together as the heat rose to post Hiroshima levels inside the camper. Aftershocks wracked their bodies as he grew soft. He rolled onto his side and took her with him, peppering her chin, her cheeks, her lids, her lips, with featherlight kisses. She lay pliant in his arms, well spent, well fucked, well loved.

He eased back, and her eye lids lifted with near catatonic laziness.

"What is it?" Her breathing had slowed, but the words still came out breathy.

"Have I told you today how much I love you?"

She stiffened beneath the hand making lazy circles on her hip. Silas didn't wait for her to answer. "It doesn't matter. I love you. And I am going to keep saying I love you every day, or every hour if I have to, until I can say it and you don't get that look in your eye like a felon who's spotted an open cell door."

"You can't keep saying that."

"Shhh." He smiled because for once her tone didn't reach out and sock him in the gut. "Oh, hotstuff. I can. I will. Until you no longer squirm when I say it, or turn green behind the gills."

"I can't love you."

Can't and *don't* were not the same word.

"But you do."

She didn't deny it, but she wouldn't confirm it either. She opened her mouth. "I…"

He saw the rest of it. The *love you* in her eyes. Felt it in the hand she laid on his chest. She wanted to say it, he was sure of it. "I love you," he said again.

"I know."

Before she could say anything they would both regret, he said, "And that's okay. You don't have to say it back. Not yet. I said I'd wait for you. I meant it."

———

"HEY THERE," JOSEPHINE SAID AS SHE CAME UP BEHIND SILAS IN the area behind the bull chutes at the Ogden rodeo in Utah. The week had whizzed by in a dizzying speed of hot sex, hard training, and long drives.

"Hey there yourself." Silas hardly looked up from the rigging bag as he pulled out two bullropes.

They were crowded in a small area about three stalls wide and one stall deep. This was the 'secure' area Maynard had promised the riders where they could store their gear before their rides. It wasn't exactly Fort Knox. The walls were made from corral panels that anyone could climb over or slip through. The kid sitting on a stool at the entrance pretty much let anyone in, which was how she'd gotten in. Rowdy was back there showing off with his newest side piece, this one short with flowing, bright red hair that almost matched the makeup surrounding his painted-on smile.

Silas leaned against the panel, one leg bent with the heel of his booted foot resting on the lower rail. Monte slid behind her to get to his bag, and she scooted next to Silas to get out of the way.

After their confrontation the week before, Monte hadn't said a word to either of them. Probably just as well. He rarely said anything she wanted to hear these days.

Silas snuck a quick kiss to the side of her cheek then went back to inspecting every inch of his bullropes for any signs of wear or fraying or sabotage. "Comet settled in for the night?"

"Finished up a few minutes ago."

He lowered the rope and caught her attention. "Look at me." When she did, he said, "You and Comet killed it tonight. Why are you so nervous?"

"I'm not nervous."

He dropped the rope on his bag and placed a hand on her cheek, his hand cold and clammy, and here he was calling her out about being nervous. He ran his thumb along her bottom lip. The one she was worrying with her teeth, until she'd worn a raw spot near the corner.

"It's not me I'm worried about," she said.

"It's okay." He wrapped her in a hug and held her tight against his chest. He smelled of fresh sweat, and old leather and determination. She was going to have a heck of a time leaving after Cheyenne. "I can't wait to get out there and show those bulls they haven't gotten the best of me. Not by a long shot."

It was then that she saw the leather thong around his neck, dipping beneath the collar of his starched, black western shirt. She raised her hand to his chest, the lump beneath his shirt hanging level with his heart.

Outlining the object with her fingertips, she immediately knew what it was. "Where did you get this?"

He held his hand over hers, trapping Toby's bear claw beneath her hand. Silas's hand was warmer now, and she liked to think she had something to do with quelling his nervousness.

"I found it in the dirt near where Toby had fallen. The leather had broken. I'm keeping it safe for him."

"Isn't that his good luck charm."

He laughed, but his humor sounded in short supply. Silas reached for the necklace as if he was going to take it off. "Maybe it's not so lucky."

She stilled his hand. "Toby's alive. Maybe without this, he wouldn't be."

He made that kind of face that reluctantly said she had a point.

The crowd in the stands cheered at something the announcer said. Then a spotter hollered over. "That's it, Foss, you're up."

He'd drawn the first bull of the evening. Josephine was almost glad. It would have been much harder to sit through a bunch of rides waiting, anticipating.

Silas chose his older bullrope, the one that had been his backup before his other one had been sliced. Like her, he much preferred not using brand new equipment on an important ride. "You going to watch from the stands?"

She suppressed the shiver at the idea. Now that the word had gotten out that she and Silas were seeing each other, the media couldn't get enough of them. Some reporter had even wanted to do an interview with the both of them earlier in the afternoon. They'd declined. But that didn't mean the cameras wouldn't find her in the stands.

God forbid, if something happened to Silas, the last thing she wanted was for her reaction, her terror, to be replayed on the ten o'clock news. "No. I'll find a spot and watch from here."

"*Foss.*"

"Coming!" Silas walked backward toward the chutes, the bells on his bullrope clacking dully as he hefted the rope to his shoulder. To her, he said, "I'll see you after the ride."

He turned to climb over the rail.

"Be safe," she said to his back.

As he threw his leg over the top of the rail, he looked back at her, tossing her a quick wink. The crowd was too loud to hear his reply, but his lips read *always*.

10

THE RAIL OF THE CHUTE WAS SLICK BENEATH SILAS'S SWEATY hand. He blanked out the noise of the crowd, rolled his head on his shoulders to try to relieve the tension building there, acutely aware of Toby's bear claw as the sharp tip dug into his sternum, as if his friend was telling him to pay attention. To be careful. To not end up in the dirt the way Toby had.

At least he knew his rope was good, and with the word getting around about what had happened, everyone had been extra vigilant, checking and rechecking their gear. He had a good feeling about this rodeo.

He took a deep breath as he settled into his hand, the jet-black bull antsy and pawing the raw earth beneath them. A fine cloud of dirt drifted into the air, tickling his nose and making him cough.

As soon as his legs hit the bull's sides, he released his grip on the rail and nodded to the gateman. The gate swung open, and Rendezvous leaped out of the chute. Silas dug his spurs into thick hide as the bull spun out into the arena, kicking his heels high.

Rendezvous had a reputation as a fierce bull to ride, but Silas had successfully ridden him before. That's how he knew when the bull dropped his big blocky head exactly what was coming.

The stutter step.

The direction change.

The immediate, kidney dislodging, spine snapping, brain-jarring shift as if the bull was trying to launch Silas into the next dimension. Pain skirted around his brain then quickly dissipated.

Silas had been ready for Rendezvous' signature move. The time off hadn't diminished his balance or loosened his grip. The tendons in his shoulder strained and flexed, but held, his bicep burning as if branded.

The buzzer went off and over the hammering of his pulse behind his eardrums, rose the hoots and hollers and stomping of feet in the stands. The ear-splitting racket penetrated his brain.

He'd done it.

He'd *fucking* done it.

Jumping free the bull, Silas ran to the chutes as the beast was herded through the end gate. He straddled the top of an empty chute, shot both fists into the air and howled at the rising moon.

The crowd got impossibly louder. The whole stadium vibrated as if an epic earthquake rocked the world. But no. It was just him. And Rendezvous. And a record-breaking score paving the road to Cheyenne.

The stands tilted, and Silas grabbed for the rail, missed, then caught. Then his stomach dropped five floors, and he knew he was going to be sick. Fucking adrenaline.

He climbed up the chute and jumping down on the other side, rattling his brain. A flash of pain. He may not be as healed as he'd thought he was. He sunk to his knees in a corner behind the chutes and retched, his abdomen heaving, until it felt like his stomach had emptied of every meal he'd ever eaten.

He collapsed on the ground, covering the vomit and the stench with a sweep of his hand through the deep dirt. With his back to the rails, he clamped his hands to his temples, trying to quell the pounding in his head.

"Ohmygod." Josephine appeared beside him. He hadn't even seen her climb over or through the panel. "Are you okay? Do you need me to call the ambulance?"

Silas raised his head. The world tipped, and Josephine went fuzzy.

She held up one hand. "How many fingers am I holding up?"

Seven. Or is that eight? He batted her hand to get it out of his face. "I'm fine. It's just the adrenaline. It's gotta go somewhere. Sometimes it's up. It's no big deal."

"I'm gonna have the paramedics come take a look, just in case."

He wasn't a kid. He was old enough to know if he needed to be examined. His anger flared, and before he was able to bank it, he took it out on her. "Jesus Christ. Can you stop mothering me for one *fucking* second?"

"You threw up. The doctor at the hosp—"

"*Enough.*" She fell back on her ass as if his anger had knocked her over. He gathered his unsteady legs beneath him. Almost going back down as he bent to pick up his hat. He brushed the dirt off on the legs of his chaps, more to give his legs a chance to steady, than the fact that he gave two shits about his hat right then. "What I need is for you to quit hovering and give me some space."

She glared up at him. If looks could kill, he'd have been filleted and drawn and quartered. Pushing to her feet, she said, "Cowboy, if it's space you want, I'll give you the whole damn universe. But you might want to grab your coat. I hear it's a bit chilly out there."

———

As Comet galloped toward the third barrel, his hooves an ear-numbing, pulse-pounding, earth-shaking staccato beneath her, Josephine tried to push Silas's words from the night before out of her mind. The crowd in the stands were a blur of color as she stood in the stirrups, her hands up Comet's neck as she focused on the third can.

Her nemesis.

She was near to the last to make her run. Cora and one of the other girls had pulled times so impressive Josephine would have to skim that third barrel tight if she had any chance of qualifying for the finals on Sunday.

A few strides away from the turn, she eased off the speed.

Stop mothering me.

Silas's words broke into her brain, and Josephine pulled on the left rein a little too hard, a little too fast. Comet tossed his head and dropped his shoulder into the turn.

Quit hovering.

Comet's left rear leg slid in the dirt, his back end almost coming out from beneath him. Josephine squeezed her calves, urging him forward. His feet scrambling for traction.

I need some space.

Comet drove Josephine's knee into the lip of the barrel. It spun in the dirt, but Josephine couldn't wait and watch to see if it fell. She used her reins and her legs, igniting Comet's turbo drive as they galloped past the finish line and out the end of the arena into the alleyway.

She pulled Comet to a stop and glanced over at Cora. Her friend gave her a thumbs up. The barrel had stayed up. Ahead of her, Silas stood by the open gate leading to the warm-up arenas, waiting for her even though they hadn't spoken since the night before.

She gave Comet's reins a little tug, breaking him out of the animated jigging. Her horse was already looking for the next barrel, the next run.

"What happened to relaxing into that third barr—"

Josephine cut Silas a scathing look. *He'd* happened. Typically, she looked forward to his critiques. He'd coached his younger sister to the junior nationals before he'd turned pro. He knew his stuff. But she was in no mood to hear it.

See? You should have laid off the men. He almost cost you that run. And for what? A few fun tumbles. A few orgasms.

They were amazing org—

Amazing orgasms won't get you to Cheyenne.

She gave Comet his head and a little leg. He'd wanted space.

"Baby," he said as she clomped on by. "*Josephine.*"

Josephine blew out a breath and Comet relaxed beneath her, settling into a nice lazy walk as they entered the outside arena so she could cool him down. Maybe Silas was right. Maybe what they both needed was room to breathe.

———

JOSEPHINE AND CORA SAT IN FOLDING CHAIRS IN THE NOSE OF HER horse trailer, their sock feet on Josephine's lower bunk. The door stood open, and a steady Ogden drizzle and a light breeze keep them from parboiling in the tin can they called home.

Cora splashed tequila into their shot glasses. Josephine's had the chip on the rim from falling on the floor after a trip down a rutted dirt road.

"To men," Cora said as they clinked their glasses together. "They're all assholes."

"Here, here." Josephine slammed the shot back, coughed and reached for the bottle. When the glasses were full again, she said, "And to Silas in particular who took assholer-y to a whole new—"

"Assholer-y?" Silas stepped up and leaned a shoulder against their open door, his hair and shoulders damp from the light rain. "I'm not sure that's a real word."

"If it's not..." Cora downed her shot, no cough, no wince. A real pro. "It should be."

Josephine tipped the bottom of her shot glass up, swallowed hard, and reached for the bottle again.

"You know you ladies have to ride tomorrow, right?"

"Who's the one mothering now?" Josephine couldn't keep the snark out of her voice, not that she tried really hard.

"Uh, oh," Cora said. "This is awkward." But instead of leaving them alone, she settled deeper into her chair, looking like she needed a big fat tub of buttery popcorn, so she could sit back and enjoy the fireworks.

"Can I come in?"

The rain had picked up, and water dripped down his face and off the end of his nose and chin. He tucked his hands deep into his pockets. Josephine almost felt sorry for him. Almost.

"Say what you came to say. Then leave." Cora wasn't one to mind her own business.

He glanced over. "Cora? Do you mind?"

"Not at all. You go right ahead and say what you're gonna say."

Silas blew out an exasperated breath. "That's not what I meant, and you know it."

Cora reached down and filled her mouth with squirt cheese. "I know." Though, with her mouth full of processed cheese, it came out sounding like *ah oh.*

Lightning lit the sky. Long, white, gnarly fingers. The thunderclap ripped through the air and Cora spilled the next pour all over the wood floor. The liquid slid through the gaps between the planks and drained onto the ground.

"Cut me some slack, Cora." Silas looked at Josephine. "Or not. I've got something I want to say, and I'll say it out here, in front of God and everyone if that's what you want me to do."

"Yes," Josephine said.

"Yes, you want me to spill my guts in front of witnesses or—"

"Yes, you can come in."

Silas climbed in, standing in the one square foot of open floor space next to the door. With the wind picking up, it was probably only slightly drier than standing outside.

"You really fucked the pooch this time, mister. You should —" Cora grabbed for the paper plate filled with Saltines. "Oh, man. You're dripping on our hors-d'oeuvres."

"Sorry." He ran his hand through his hair, slinging water over the bunks and them without even trying. "Look Josephine—"

"Ooh, look." Cora had the attention span of a squirrel on speed. "It's that new heeler from Saskatchewan. I've never had a Canuck. I wonder if it's true what they say about them..." Cora grabbed her slicker and held it over her head, shoved the tequila in her armpit, and dashed past Silas into the rain. "You hoo! Hey, stud! Drinks on me!"

Despite being soaked to the skin, Silas chuckled. "She's a trip."

"Tell me about it." Josephine pulled her feet off her bunk and waved a hand at Cora's vacated chair. "Have a seat."

The wind had shifted, and it was drenching the inside of the trailer. Silas closed the door, and Josephine reached behind her for her big six-volt battery lantern. She turned it on and swiveled the head, aiming it at the ceiling. The battery was weak, and the dim, yellow light was hardly better than nothing at all.

In the dwindling light, Silas looked even more tired than he had the past few days and just because he didn't want her to worry about him, didn't mean she could turn her concern for him off like a switch.

"I came to apologize."

"Apology accepted." She didn't hesitate, though she also wasn't in any kind of mood to talk about it.

Silas looked at her, his head cocked as if he were trying to puzzle her out. "Your words said *apology accepted*. Your tone pretty much said get the hell out."

She held out the shot glass to him. It was mostly full. "You want this?"

He took the shot and threw the liquid into the back of his throat, thumping his chest with his fist and breathing fire. "Jesus. How the hell is a woman as tiny as you still vertical?"

"Practice," she said. You didn't run a season on the circuit with Cora Hayes and not learn how to hold your liquor. Her father would be appalled. Naughty grandma would give Josephine a high five.

The spot of light on the roof of the trailer decreased by half, and the intensity of the rain doubled to an almost deafening decibel. Silas reached for her hand, and she let him take it. Water dripped down his arm and seeped into her jeans.

When he spoke, he had to raise his voice to be heard over the drumming rain. "I really am sorry, babe. That was most definitely an assholer-y thing for me to have said. I know you were just worried about me, and I shouldn't have taken it out on you."

She smiled at his use of her made-up word. Loved that he could make fun of himself. "And I'm sorry if you felt like I was smothering you."

Silas didn't carry all the blame. Everyone getting sick or hurt, first Silas, then her mother, and now Toby, had sent her reeling. None of it within her control. She couldn't do anything for her mother or Toby, but she wanted to do something for Silas.

A little too much something, apparently.

"It's okay, I kn—"

"No. It's not okay. Maybe we need to take a step back—"

"Nope." Silas's fingers tightened around hers. "I don't like the way that sounds. Not even a little bit. Look, I changed my mind. Smother me. I don't need air or space or to breathe. None of that is important. All I want to do with you is move forward."

"We both know this can't go anywhere. Maybe it's best we put some distance between ourselves. Being together for the time we have left is only going to make saying goodbye that much harder."

"Nothing says we have to say good—"

"Stop." Josephine stood, wanting to pace but there was nowhere to go. The walls of the stuffy trailer closed in on her, and Silas standing made her even more claustrophobic. "This conversation is going in circles. I don't want to argue with you, I just..."

She didn't know what to say to make him give up. The tequila finally hit her system, and between the liquor and the exhaustion, her thoughts kept whirling around in no particular direction. She gave him a look, pleading with him for mercy. She didn't want to say goodbye, but they both wanted different things out of life.

He shook his head and sighed, the grim expression on his face softened around his eyes. "Come here." He held out his arms, and she walked into them, settling her arms around his waist and her head on his warm, damp chest. He pressed a kiss to her forehead, and let her go. Opening the door, he glanced back at her and said, "This isn't over."

She wasn't getting into this with him again. "I'm truly sorry, Silas."

"You're sorry." The disappointment in his voice hit her

harder than her father's had that time he'd caught her sneaking out to a barn party in high school.

Her throat tightened, and before she could say anything else that would confuse the matter like, *don't go*, she said, "Yeah. I'm sorry."

"Me, too."

He stepped out of the trailer, the rain had let up some, but he'd be soaked by the time he made a dash for his camper.

"Silas."

He stopped and turned.

She gripped the door handle to keep herself from following. "Are you really okay?"

"My head is fine. My heart..." His lips turned down at the ends, and he swallowed hard and said, "...not so much."

Silas's world had tilted off its axis, and it had nothing to do with alcohol or his concussion, and everything to do with a woman.

Josephine.

The same woman who'd told him last week that she was backing away.

The same woman who'd avoided him all week.

The same woman who'd showed up last night at his camper and took him, slow and deep, without saying a word.

The same woman who'd vanished by the time he'd woken up.

Tension knotted the muscles along his spine, and his heart felt like she'd raked him with sharpened spurs. Right then, he didn't know much. What he did know, was if the bulls didn't kill him, Josephine certainly would.

At the pay phone next to the Cheyenne rodeo office, Silas dialed the operator and got the number for Toby's hospital back in Salinas.

After connecting with his room, the phone was picked up on

the fourth ring. "Ye—" Toby coughed up something that sounded wet and thick. He spat. "Yeah."

"It's me." The tension eased from around Silas's chest at the sound of his friend's voice. Silas put his finger in his other ear to cut out the background noise. He didn't know if it was the connection that was so bad, or if Toby was so weak that he couldn't speak up.

"You made it. Ho-ly shiiit. *Cheyenne*."

There were a lot of things Silas wanted to say to Toby, but he held back, not wanting to make the man sick with all the sappy sentiment, so he only said, "You should be here."

"Next year." And it sounded like Toby meant it. "Doc says if I take care of myself, I could be back on the bulls come spring."

"That's good news, man. The best."

"Yeah. You sound thrilled. If I didn't know any better, I'd have thought your best friend died, but that's me, so I know that's not true. Spill."

"Look, I gotta go. I just wanted to check on you and—"

"Bullshit. The rodeo doesn't start for a couple more hours."

The numbers on the telephone dial blurred and his head swam. He really needed to get more sleep. Silas leaned against the pay phone, resting his arm on the top and pinching the bridge of his nose to stave off the building pressure behind his eyes. "Josephine's pretty much called it off."

"Called what off."

"Us. Whatever the hell it was we had going on between us."

"I know you liked her, but man, this is Cheyenne. Don't let her steal your mojo. There are plenty of ladies out there that would be more than happy to shine your buckle if you give them a chance."

"Jesus Christ, Tobe. It isn't like that. You don't understand."

Toby was quiet for a second and Silas was about to ask if he was still on the line when his friend said, "Try me."

Fuck. Silas looked around making sure no one was anywhere near. The last thing he wanted was anyone hearing—

"Oh shit," Toby said as if the words *love sick* flashed in bright red neon over Silas's heart. "You love her."

Silas couldn't tell if Toby was awed, or repulsed.

Before Silas could answer, Toby said, "Let me give you some advice."

Silas had sunk to an unfathomable level of desperation if he was considering taking relationship advice from Toby. Don't get him wrong, Toby was a great guy. Just crappy boyfriend material...according to a long line of women. "This should be good."

"Hear me out."

Silas pressed his back against the exterior wall of the office, and the tilting stalls across from him seemed to right themselves.

"Put this woman out of your mind—"

"If I could do that, I wouldn't be so fucked up right now."

"You didn't let me finish. Put this woman out of your mind until tomorrow night. Twenty-four hours. You think you can manage that, buddy?" Toby didn't wait for him to reply. "You've worked too hard, risked too much, to lose your focus now. But come tomorrow night, you find her, and you do or say whatever you must to make her yours. You got that?"

Silas chuckled. Sounded like a solid plan. "Got it."

Silas had to add more money which gave him just enough time to fill Toby in on the sabotage to the bullropes. When the phone wanted even more money, Silas said, "I really gotta go this time, but as soon as this is over I'm coming to see you."

"Don't worry about me. I'm not going anywhere for awhile. You worry about hog-tying that woman so tight that she never gets away."

Hmmm. A little rope sounded intriguing.

Silas shook his head, but all that managed to do was make the stalls tilt again. "Talk to you soon."

"I'm gonna be watching. Don't make me embarrassed to say I know you."

"Fuck you."

Silas heard Toby's laugh before the phone cut them off.

The ride. Then the girl. Who'd of thought Toby, of all people, would be the voice of reason?

STUPID, STUPID, STUPID, STUPID.

Stupid.

Stupid.

"You're the most bitchin' woman I know." Cora and her horse Panache walked with Josephine and Comet to a patch of grass past the parking lot. They had a few minutes to let the horses stretch their legs and graze before they had to warm the horses up. "I wanna be like you when I grow up. You're so friggin' cool."

Josephine's stomach felt like someone had tied it in a constrictor knot and yanked it tight. And the most insane thing was, she'd done it to herself. Teach her to listen to the devil on her shoulder.

"There was nothing bitchin' about it. In fact, I think I want to throw up."

"Maybe you're pregnant."

"What? No. Definitely not. It's my conscience telling me I screwed over a good guy I really care about."

"It wasn't like he stopped you. You're the one who said it was the banging-est sex you'd ever had. Sounds like he was on board and—"

"*Cora.* Would you listen to yourself?"

"What? He's hot."

"Yeah, but he's so much more than that. He's thoughtful, and sincere, and loving, and considerate, and for some unfathomable reason, he thinks he loves me, even though I've treated him like shit."

"Well, the treating him like shit is new, so..."

Josephine cut her a look that said *you're supposed to be on my side.*

"You went to him. You jumped his bones. He liked it. You liked it. Nothing wrong with that. It's not like it's the fifties anymore."

"Yeah. I jumped him *after* I said we were done. He probably hates me now."

"Silas doesn't hate you. Besides, it's a woman's prerogative to change her mind."

"Not like that. I don't want to be *that* woman." They stopped at the patch of grass, and the horses dropped their heads and started shearing the tops off the blades. "I don't know what came over me."

"Lust." Cora nodded her head with certainty. "You've seen that ass, right?"

"Cora," Josephine warned.

"And the way those chaps frame his package—"

"*Cora.*"

"*Whaaaat?*"

Josephine stared off into the distance as one of the trailers carrying more roughstock, steers it looked like, pulled into the parking lot. "It's more than that. I mean if we had met a couple years from now, or if he wasn't looking for a way off the circuit, then maybe..."

Cora nudged Josephine's foot with the tip of her boot. Her voice soft and serious when she said, "No. I get it, girl. You've got it bad for him, and it's scaring the hell out of you."

"I don't want to hurt him."

"Don't worry about him. He's a big boy. It's you I'm worried about."

"Me?" Comet bumped her with his shoulder, and she took a step aside, to let him get at the grass near her feet. Apparently, the grass was greener under the boots.

"You're so caught up on following these rigid rules you'd set up for yourself at the beginning of the season. Frankly, you need to loosen up. You want to bend, not break." Cora tossed her head toward the barn. "Come on. Let's take the horses the long way around, then back through the trailers so we can start getting ready. I don't know about you, but I've got a barrel race to win."

"Not if I win it first."

Cora laughed. "On that walking gluestick?"

Comet lifted his head, blowing out his nose and coating Cora's arm in horse snot.

"Ewh." Cora wiped her arm. "See? Males are assholes."

Josephine laughed and tugged on Comet's lead rope. "You did just insult him."

They followed Cora and Panache around the perimeter of the parking area then cut back through the camper and trailer lot.

"What was that?" Cora stopped. Panache stopped, and Josephine bumped into a dappled copper horse rump.

Panache turned his head and gave her a lazy blink. Josephine patted his backside and stepped up beside Cora. "What's what?"

Cora was bent over at the waist. Her head upside down as if she were looking for an empty stall in the women's restroom. Josephine bent over and looked under the trailer was well.

"Did you see that?" Cora said.

The trailer shifted as if someone had climbed inside. "I didn't see anything."

"Come on." Cora tied Panache to an empty stock trailer, and Josephine did the same with Comet.

"What are we doing?"

"That's Monte's trailer. Someone just went in there."

"Yeah," Josephine said, "Probably Monte."

"Uh, uh. Monte's chillin' at the Chop House with some of the guys. And his truck's still gone. Maybe whoever is in there is trying to cut Monte's rope, like he did the rest."

"Silas thinks Monte's the one who—"

"Nope." Cora grabbed her arm and dragged her along like an old hag bound for the glue factory. "Monte's an ass, but he's no killer."

Josephine dug her heels in. "Would you stop?"

Cora stopped but didn't loosen her grip. "We can't let him get away."

"And how do you expect to stop him? If it is even him. And if it is, we know he's got a knife. He probably won't be afraid to use it."

"You go get help, then." Cora dropped Josephine's arm and started creeping toward the trailer. "And I'll make sure he doesn't get away."

"Cora."

Cora tiptoed to the back of the trailer.

"*Cora.*" Josephine whisper-yelled.

Waving her hands, Cora shushed her. And gestured toward the rodeo office. Right. Help. Josephine needed to get help before Cora did something stupid.

———

SILAS SPRINTED FOR THE BACK LOT, HIS BOOTS BEATING A STEADY rhythm on the asphalt. He'd sent Josephine into the office to have Maynard alert the rodeo security while he ran to help Cora.

The women shouldn't have split up like that, leaving one to confront a potentially dangerous man.

Silas's boots slid as he came around the corner of Monte's trailer. Someone was pounding on the inside of the door. Cora was sitting on the steps, her back braced against the door, her belt looped from the doorknob to the grip handle on the side of the camper.

"L-l-let me out." *Bam, bam, bam.* "Open this f-fucking door."

Cora smiled up at Silas. "I'll give you three guesses."

He only needed one. *Rowdy Boyd.* "That sonofabitch."

Silas leaned against someone's faded red pickup and tried to catch his breath. His head pounded as if a herd of Brahman were stampeding through his brain. He squeezed his eyes shut, but that only made him dizzy.

"L-let me out." Rowdy pounded again.

After catching his breath, Silas stepped up to the trailer and hammered his fist against the camper door. It shook on its frame. "I'm happy to let you out, Rowdy. How much damage do you think I can do before the sheriff's boys get here, asshole?"

Rowdy stopped pounding.

Silas thought so.

"Get me o-out of here."

"Not until you tell me what you're doing in Monte's trailer."

"I needed to borrow—"

Silas made the sound in the back of his throat he'd used as a kid when his dog had tried to dig under the fence. "Try again."

Silence. It dragged on. A wave of dizziness made Silas sway, and he latched onto the trailer handle for support.

Through the door, Rowdy said, "L-ook, man. No one was s-supposed to get h-hurt."

Silas yanked Cora's belt off the knob and threw open the

camper door. Rowdy stood in the entrance, his eyes wide and an *oh fuck* frown on his face. Silas reached in and dragged him down the two steps. With a shove, he rammed Rowdy against the side of the camper, a hollow thump as Rowdy's head dented the thin metal siding.

"No one was supposed to get hurt? *No one was supposed to get hurt?*" Silas hollered, his vocal cords stretched and strained. "What the fuck is that supposed to mean?"

Silas grabbed him by the front of his shirt. Cora tore at Silas's arm trying to pull him off Rowdy, but he ignored her. Rowdy went out of focus, but Silas managed to blink him clear. He shoved the bastard against the camper again.

"Easy man." Rowdy said, his stutter diminished with his agitation. "When Navarro got knocked out, that rope busting probably saved his l-life."

Silas saw red. Sound blanked out. Rowdy's lips moved but hell if Silas knew if the clown was stuck in a stutter or if Silas was so hopped up on adrenaline he couldn't hear anything.

It didn't matter. The shit-head nearly killed Silas's best friend. He landed a punch to Rowdy's face. Goliath hammering David. Rowdy cratered. One second he was standing, the next he was sprawled out on the hot asphalt.

Stupid prick.

One hit wasn't enough. Bending down, Silas scooped up fist-fuls of cotton T-shirt and reared back to take another swing. Silas heard the holler a nano-second before Cora landed on his back. Her legs wrapped around his waist, her arms around his neck.

"Silas, Silas. Cut it out. You want to get arrested, too, you big dummy?"

He stood, and between his lingering dizziness and Cora's added weight, he staggered back a couple steps. "Okay, okay." He peeled her arms from around his neck, and she dropped to her feet.

Behind them, Josephine and Maynard and a couple of deputies rushed over.

"What's going on?" One of the deputies asked. He was clean-cut with reflective sunglasses that he propped up on his broad forehead.

"I caught him breaking into Monte's trailer." Cora waved a hand in Rowdy's direction.

Rowdy moaned and rolled around on the ground as he started to regain consciousness, the blood from an obviously broken nose marring the white face paint.

"And what happened to his face?"

"He tripped," Silas said.

The deputy cut his eyes to Cora. Clearly, he wasn't buying Silas's story.

"Rowdy is rather clumsy." Cora threw on one of her *aw-shucks* smiles on her face that usually got her a free drink or two at the bar. "He is a clown after all."

"He cut the bullropes and sabotaged the rides. He admitted as much." Silas stepped closer to Rowdy, wanting nothing more than to drive the tip of his boot into Rowdy's ribs for Toby's sake. Who was the idiot who said you couldn't kick a man while he was down? Silas couldn't think of a better time to do it.

The second deputy patted Rowdy down for weapons and found a switchblade stuffed in one of his socks. He rolled him onto his stomach and cuffed him, then manhandled him to his feet.

"Come on," the first deputy said, indicating Silas and Cora. "We'll head down to the station for questioning."

"Ho, now." Maynard stepped in. He even took the cigar out of his mouth so he could speak clearly. He must have been serious. "Look, deputy. I know you're just doing your job, but Foss here is one of the stars of the show. He's like the fourth Beatle. You can't have a show without all the stars, and I've got the biggest show of the year going on, starting in the next couple hours. Take Rowdy in and leave these two. I'll personally drive them down to the station when they've finished competing tonight."

Sunglasses looked at the second deputy who shrugged his shoulders as if to say *your call*. To Maynard, Sunglasses said, "I'll tell the Sheriff to be expecting you."

They took Rowdy to a Black and White that another one of the deputies had driven over. The nosebleed had slowed along the way. They dumped Rowdy on the back seat, the door open, his feet hanging out while someone jogged off to get a rag to help staunch the rest of the bleeding.

Josephine stepped up to Silas, and despite what had happened the night before, he wrapped his arm around her shoulders and pressed a kiss to the side of her head, glad that she was safe. Glad that they were all going to be safe now.

She took his hand and brushed her thumb over his skinned knuckles. "How's the hand?"

He flexed and extended his fingers. His pulse throbbed in his knuckles, and the movement was slow and stiff, but no broken bones popped or cracked. "It'll do."

"That was a stupid thing to do. If you'd broken your hand on Rowdy's face, you wouldn't have been able to ride tonight."

After what she'd pulled last night, he should be angry, not grinning down at her and loving the flash of vinegar in her eyes. "Awh, you do still care."

He meant it as a joke. Meant to make Josephine laugh, but instead, red rimmed her eyes, and she blinked fast, swiping at her cheek, which only seemed to make her madder. "Of course, I care. Last night...I never would have..." She glanced away, her cheeks flushed, but then she met his gaze. "I never would have done what I did, if you weren't important to me."

He knew that. That's why none of this made any sense. They belonged together. He had no doubt of that, but convincing Josephine was proving harder than he'd ever expected.

A station wagon drove up. Monte and a few of the other bull riders piled out of the vehicle.

"What's going on?" Monte said.

Monte approached one of the deputies. Silas leaned in and said to Josephine, "Have dinner with me tonight. After your ride. We'll go into town and talk."

She took a step back. "I promised to go out with the girls tonight. It's our last night before—"

"No, Josephine." He dropped his voice so it wouldn't carry. "It's *our* last night."

Monte glanced into the back of the deputy's car and hitched a thumb at Rowdy over his shoulder. "What the hell happened to him?"

Cora walked up to Monte. "Silas happened to him. We caught him in your trailer. It's him. He's the one who's been cutting the ropes."

"Why would he do that?" Monte directed his attention to Silas, but Silas ignored the question. He had more important things on his mind besides some two-bit, washed-up, no-good, bullfighter.

"Then meet me after you're done." Silas kept hold of her hand even as she tried to pull it free. "I don't care what time."

Monte walked over, reached inside the car, and jerked Rowdy out, holding him up until his toes almost came off the ground. "Why would you do that? What is wrong with you?"

"Dinner's not a good idea," Josephine said. "The finals are tomorrow. I rode hard all season. None of it matters if I blow it on the last ride. I need a clear head. Not to rehash our relationship. I've made my decision. You need to respect that."

Respect that. How could Silas respect it when he didn't even understand it? He loved her. Even though she hadn't said it back, he knew she loved him, too. She wouldn't have done what she had last night, he wouldn't have felt what he'd felt, if she didn't.

Monte voice rose and cut through the small groups of curious people who had gathered around. "I knew there was a reason I hated your punk ass."

Sunglasses stopped his conversation with Maynard and hurried over to the cruiser. "Put him down or I'll haul your ass to jail, too."

Monte didn't even spare the deputy a glance. His focus was on Rowdy who was trying to say something, but Silas was too far away to hear what. But Silas was too far to see Monte's face flush with anger and watch him shake the deputy off like he was a weak, runt calf. "You cut ropes. For *attention*? For *pussy*?"

Monte reared back to land his own punch.

The second deputy grabbed him from behind and pinned his arms behind his back. "You're under arrest."

Josephine's hand flew to her mouth, and she looked back at Silas. Right then, he didn't care what sick, messed up reason Rowdy had for trying to get attention, to make himself look good, all Silas cared about was talking some sense into an unreasonable woman.

"Tomorrow night. After the rodeo then. We'll talk." He wasn't asking this time.

Josephine took a half-step back. "I really need to get Comet warmed up." She took a couple more steps back, and he was forced to drop her hand.

"Promise me," he said.

"Tomorrow night."

She turned and walked away. Cora caught up with her as the deputies stuffed Rowdy and Monte into the back of the car. *Tomorrow night.* She'd agreed.

But she hadn't promised.

12

―――

AT THE END OF THE CROWDED BAR, SILAS RAISED HIS HAND, AND the bartender brought him his third whiskey. Or was it his fourth? His head spun, but he couldn't tell if it was from the alcohol, the after-effects of the concussion, or the hour of questioning back at the Sheriff's office.

"That drink's on me." A tall skinny kid said to the bartender, pointing to Silas's drink. "Gimme whatever you have on tap."

Silas had seen the kid around the circuit. Some hayseed from Kansas or Idaho or some such place. Bob, he thought his name was. Silas had talked to him a few times. Given him some pointers. Nice enough kid. But Silas was in no mood to make nice.

The crowd shifted, and he got a good look at Josephine and Cora, a couple of the other can chasers, and some of Maynard's drill team riders crowded around a table near the dance floor. Drinking and laughing. A never-ending supply of men in tight jeans and big buckles doing drive-bys, asking them to dance, or sitting and buying one or two a drink.

Some asshole, rodeo wannabe took Josephine's hand and

leaned in and whispered something into her ear. Silas took a sip of his whiskey instead of barging over there and ripping the guy's hand off his body and beat him with it.

"That's a long face for a guy at the top of the leaderboard." The kid took the empty stool next to Silas.

"Look, Bob now's not the—"

"Ron," the kid said with that same star-struck smile he had the first time they'd been introduced. "The name's Ron."

Bob. Ron. Three letters. An 'o' in the middle. Silas had been close.

"Thanks for the drink, but I'm sitting alone at a bar for a reason." Silas gripped the glass tighter as Wannabe led Josephine to the dance floor and rubbed his belt buckle against her hard enough to rub the silver plating off. "Asshole."

"I buy you a drink, and I'm an asshole?"

Jesus Christ. Silas couldn't win. "Not you." He pointed to the dance floor. The song had ended, but Wannabe kept Josephine out on the floor waiting for the next song to start up. "Him."

The kid's smile got bigger, and Silas saw a gap in his front teeth wide enough to drive a hundred head through. "Him who? All I see is a beautiful woman with a world class ass, and a rocking rack that I'd kill to—"

Silas slammed his glass on the counter, shutting the kid up. It wasn't the kid's fault. The kid didn't know Josephine belonged to Silas. Still, Silas didn't need to be reminded of what was probably running through Wannabe's head. Besides, Silas could read it on the douchebag's face. Silas shook the spilled whiskey off his hand and stumbled to his feet.

The kid caught him by the arm, but Silas waved him off. Dancing with Wannabe was more than *drinks with the girls.*

He shouldered his way to the dance floor as a slow Waylon Jennings song blasted through the juke box's speakers. Wannabe pulled Josephine closer, her eyes going wide as his hands slid down the curve of her ass. She pushed against his chest, but he was a big man. Almost as big as Silas. Wannabe nuzzled her neck, his meaty paws squeezing her flesh.

Silas tapped the guy on his shoulder when all he wanted to do was bury his fist into the guy's smug face.

"Buzz off," the guy said, not bothering to look up.

"What do you want?" Josephine didn't sound happy to see him. Her eyes didn't light, they narrowed.

"I'm cutting in."

Wannabe lifted his head from where he'd had it buried in her hair and met Silas's glare with one of his own. Wannabe's jaw was thick and square like a bulldog. Silas probably would bust his hand on the guy's jaw if he threw a punch, but it would be worth it to knock the cocky smile off the man's face.

"Go find your own woman," Wannabe said.

"This *is* my woman."

Wannabe dropped his hands from Josephine's ass and took a step back, not as if he were going to run, but as if he welcomed the fight. A couple bumped into the back of Silas as they danced by, but he ignored them.

Silas widened his stance and put a little bend in his knees, ready deck the guy if he made a move. "Show me what—"

Cora squeezed between him and Wannabe, taking the guy by the hand and dragging him to another part of the dance floor. "Trust me," she said to Wannabe, "you don't want in the middle of them."

Josephine crossed her arms over her chest. "I'm not your woman."

"The hell you're not. What are you doing with him?"

"It's called dancing."

She glared. He glared back. The song ended, and the dance floor cleared, leaving him and Josephine to their standoff.

He stepped closer. She refused to back away. Leaning in, he

whispered in her ear, "You can deny me all you want, but you can't deny last night. That was all you, hotstuff." He breathed in her scent. She smelled of hay and horses. And another man's cologne. "Now get your things I'm taking you back—"

"I said, we were done, Silas. I meant it."

"Oh, no baby. We're certainly not—"

By the set of her jaw and the spit of fire in her eyes, Silas couldn't tell if she wanted to deck him or jump him.

Monte stepped over, his hand on Silas's shoulder. "Don't do this here."

Silas glanced around. The band had returned to the stage to start their next set, people were talking in groups and clusters, but most everyone's attention was riveted on the dance floor. On them. On him.

"Don't make this worse than it already is." As soon as the words dropped from Monte's mouth, Silas knew they were true, and it chapped his ass that Monte Shaw was right.

He shifted his gaze back to Josephine. Embarrassment flushed her cheeks and disgust twisted her lips. What the fuck had he done? He reached out to her. "Babe, I'm so—"

She shook her head and stepped away. The room spun, and the first chords of the band echoed in his brain. Monte clapped Silas's shoulder. "It's over."

Silas didn't know if Monte meant the conversation or the relationship. Both, if Silas had read Josephine right. Monte ushered Silas to his truck and pointed the old Chevy in the direction of the rodeo grounds. The streets were full of people in town for the rodeo, using any excuse to party. Monte weaved his way through the parking lot dodging pedestrians.

The laughs and hoots and hollers drifted in through the open windows. Silas's head spun, and the streetlights blurred into blinding stars. What the hell was wrong with him?

Silas pressed the heels of his hand to his eyes. "Why'd you step in?"

"I'm not a complete asshole."

Silas huffed out a harsh laugh and rested his head against the back of the seat. "Since when?" The world tilted and twirled, and he closed his eyes.

Monte chuckled, but he didn't say anything as he gunned the engine and raced down the drag.

Back at the rodeo grounds, Monte put a shoulder under Silas's arm and helped him to his camper. "Christ, Foss. How much did you drink tonight?"

"Naw tha mu," Silas slurred. *Not that much.* Maybe he should have had some food to sop up all that alcohol. But when your heart feels like it had been lassoed with barbed wire and ripped out of your chest, it kind of did a number on the appetite.

"Hey, Chet," Monte called out as he propped Silas up against the side of his camper. "Help me dump Silas's drunk ass into bed."

The two men wrestled Silas into his camper with a lot of cussing and name calling. They poured him into the bed over the dinette. He could still smell Josephine on his sheets.

"Brother," Monte said, "You seriously need to air this place out."

"No lie." Chet rubbed a finger under his nose then yanked off Silas's boots.

"Screw the both of you."

"Sleep it off." Monte grabbed a pillow from somewhere and threw it at Silas's face. Silas fumbled the catch and tucked the pillow under his pounding head.

Monte clomped down the steps about to close the door when Silas said, "I'm glad they dropped the charges." Mostly the words came out un-slurred.

"And here I thought you didn't like me."

"I don't. I just want to know that when I win that belt buckle tomorrow night, I've won it fair and square."

Monte laughed. "Now look who's the asshole."

Monte slammed the door, but he and Chet must not have walked far off because Silas heard Monte say, "You can tell your boss he doesn't have to worry about his precious daughter dating a bull rider anymore."

"Why's that?"

Silas smelled tobacco smoke. One of them must have lit up.

"'Cuz Foss screwed the pooch tonight. You should have seen it." Monte's voice started fading as they walked away. "It was a thing of beauty."

"What the fuck, man?" Chet sounded disgusted. Whether it was because of what Monte had said or what Silas had done, Silas would never know.

Silas was disgusted, too. With himself. *What the fuck* was right.

He hadn't just screwed the pooch he'd...he'd...the words wouldn't come. His thoughts muddied as his heartbeat took up residence in his head. Pain radiated around his skull and his scalp felt stretched like a water balloon right before it bursts.

He rolled out of bed and stumbled to the cabinet where he stored his aspirin. Catching his balance on the counter, he ripped the top off with his teeth and poured some into his hand. The pills blurred, and he couldn't tell if he had two or four.

He popped the bitter pills into his mouth. Four. Dry swallowing, he choked on one then managed to produce enough spit to get it down at least part way. He hoped like hell he felt better in the morning. He had a buckle, and more importantly, a woman, to win.

If it wasn't already too late.

THE LAST DAY OF THE CHEYENNE RODEO WAS ELECTRIC. THE excitement, tension, and nervousness hung in the air as thick and cloying as the Houston humidity in the summer. Today, the laughs seemed louder, the sun seemed brighter, and the crowds seemed bigger.

Or maybe that was just Silas's massive hangover talking.

He took a gulp of his fourth cup of coffee of the day, washing down another dose of aspirin as he headed back to the rodeo office beneath the stands to check which bull he'd drawn for the finals.

A small crowd had gathered around the bulletin board. Riders and spectators. Usually he'd work his way to the front and move on with his day, but Silas hung back, resting a shoulder against a support column and crossing his feet at the ankles, not in the mood to fight his way to the board.

A kid walked up to him, couldn't have been more than seven or eight, with a pen and a rodeo program in his hand.

"Can I have your autograph?" The kid had the whole get up. The too large straw Stetson, the scuffed boots, the baby Wranglers and the leather chaps with the fringe on the sides, and a big plastic chromed out belt buckle with a bull rider on the front.

Silas reached for the program and the pen. "Do you know who I am?"

The kid nodded his head, pushing up the brim of his hat so he could see better. "Yeah, you're my favorite. My daddy says Thrasher is unrideable."

The coffee turned bitter on his tongue when the kid reminded him of the bull that had almost killed his best friend. It was kind of an odd thing for the kid to say, but Silas didn't pay much attention, after all, Thrasher had been pulled from the roughstock string and wasn't expected back until the indoor season started in the fall. "Oh, yeah? What do you think?"

"You can ride him."

Silas scribbled his name on the program and handed it back to the kid and forced a smile. "Better believe it."

The kid ran off, catching up with a young couple watching from the line at one of the concession stands. Silas tipped his hat, and the father gave him a nod.

"How ya doin'?" A hand clapped Silas on the shoulder, and he turned to see Monte.

The words hit him like a loaded question. Maybe it was that devilish spark in Monte's eyes. "I'm fine." If he said it enough and the aspirin ever kicked in, it might actually be somewhere close to the truth.

"You haven't seen your draw yet."

"I was waiting for the crowds to clear." He glanced over at the bulletin board, and if anything, the crowd had only gotten bigger. "Save me the trouble and tell me. You're going to bust a nut if you don't spit it out."

"No, friend. This you gotta see for yourself."

Friend my ass. Silas tossed his coffee into a nearby trashcan and worked his way to the front of the crowd. He ran his finger down the line of draws.

Thrasher.

Silas waited for the burst of adrenaline, for the blood to heat in his veins for his heart to beat faster and his chest to feel three sizes too small. But he felt...nothing. Then the anger started creeping in.

Masking his expression, he turned to Monte and gave him a twitch of a smile. "Piece of cake."

Silas shouldered his way through the crowd as his anger built and built. At the rodeo office, he shoved through the door and went straight to the small room at the back that Maynard had taken over for the duration. He didn't bother knocking.

He stepped around some guy in the office and planted his palms in the middle of Maynard's desk, his face inches from a greedy man he'd grown to despise over the years. "What the fuck are you thinking?"

Maynard glanced over Silas's shoulder and said to the other man. "If you'll excuse us."

The door closed, and Maynard shifted his unlit cigar from one side of his mouth to the other.

Silas yanked it from his mouth and threw it against the wall. "Navarro's not even out of the hospital yet, and you're letting that bull back in the string?"

Maynard leaned back in the chair. "Thrasher's a star in his own right. A big draw. People come to see him as much as they come to see the riders."

Silas stood, paced to the door and then back again. "So that's what this is about? Money? That bull is going to kill someone someday."

With a one-shouldered shrug, Maynard dug a new cigar from the top drawer of his desk and cut off the end.

"And now I'm riding him, in the finals at Cheyenne. The top rider against the top bull. Tell me to my face you didn't rig this, that this isn't just one of your ploys to boost attendance."

This time, Maynard did light up. He drew on one end of the fat cigar until the other end burned red and bright. He leaned back in his chair, resting his boots on the scarred desktop. Through a haze of smoke, Maynard said, "It's the luck of the draw."

Silas slammed his hand on top of the desk. "Bullshit." The pounding of his pulse only made his headache worse, a sharp, stabbing behind his eyes as if someone was jabbing an icepick in his eye socket.

"No one's forcing you to ride." Maynard stood and pulled the stogy out of his mouth. "I'm sure Monte and the other boys would love a shot at the prize money."

Silas clenched his teeth, fighting the pain as well as his fury. "You're a greedy, rotten, bastard, you know that?"

Maynard smiled as if Silas had given him the keys to the Vegas Strip. "Now get out. We both have jobs to do."

————

I'M NOT YOUR WOMAN. HOW HAD SHE EVEN LET THAT LIE OUT OF her mouth? She was his. He was hers. And she was damn tired of denying it.

That morning, alone in her trailer, Josephine had woken up with a whole new determination. Determination to find a way to stay on the circuit, to stay with Silas and her friends, and to live her life on her terms.

All she had to do was win tonight.

Before her mother's stroke, she'd been planning to buy a new rig with the prize money, but she'd made do all season with what she had. She didn't need a fancy trailer to make her horse run faster, or a more comfortable bed to help her sleep better.

She needed Silas.

With the prize money, she could afford to pay someone to help with her mother's recovery. Not that her father couldn't afford to pay for the help, it was that he *wouldn't* pay for the help. Not when he had a dutiful daughter who could do it. So, she'd win, and she'd go home and help with her mother, but when the indoor season started up in the fall, she'd find help for her father and be back on the circuit, back with Silas.

Then, when it came time for Silas to hang up his bullrope and start his own roughstock ranch, well, they'd figure something out. It would work. It had to.

She'd wanted to find Silas, but this was a big night for both of them. They both needed to concentrate. They both needed to win. They would have plenty of time to talk after the rodeo.

She had it all planned out. Grab Comet for their run, cool him out fast, then watch Silas's ride from the chutes. When it was all over, they'd celebrate.

Naked.

13

JOSEPHINE HOPPED UP ON COMET, THE ADRENALINE ALREADY spiking through her system. Her horse jigged beneath her, feeding off her natural high. She went with the motion. Comet's muscles knotted, and Josephine knew her horse was as amped and ready as he was ever going to be.

He had the speed. They had the skill.

They could win it all.

Cora and Panache galloped out of the back of the arena, finishing with the time to beat. Josephine didn't have time to congratulate her on a fantastic run before she was given the green light to go.

Aiming her horse down the alley, she gave him his head and her heels. He leaped forward, all muscle and heart.

If heart were all it took to win, Comet would be unbeatable.

They galloped toward the first barrel, his mane and her hair flying, her eyes watering from the wind and speed. He turned around the first barrel, smoother and closer than he'd ever taken it before, his hooves finding traction in the thick dirt, and she knew he'd shaved thousands of a second off their regular time.

Comet raced toward the second barrel almost on autopilot.

Comet knew his job. Knew the pattern. Like Silas had said, all she had to do was trust him and stay out of his way. Out of the second turn, if she went by the deafening roar of the crowd, she'd post the time to beat. On the approach to the third and final barrel, Comet dug in deep, the dirt flying. The thunderous beat of his hooves hitting the ground as he pushed himself, giving her everything he had.

The third barrel came up quick. Too quick.

Relax in the turn. Let him do his job. Silas's words echoed in her head. But Comet was coming in too hot, and he wasn't slowing down.

He was going to overshoot the can.

Josephine stiffened and pulled on the inside rein. A little too fast. A little too hard. She tried to feed rein back to him, but it was already too late.

Comet dumped his shoulder into the turn, and his rear legs spun out from under him. Just like they'd had in Calgary. And just like in Calgary, her knee crashed into the barrel. It didn't spin and teeter, it slammed into the dirt.

Tears sprung to her eyes as she raced across the finish line. Comet jigged proudly after she pulled him up past the alley. He didn't understand that they'd have a five-second penalty. He didn't understand that they'd lost.

What *she'd* lost or how she'd failed.

All her hard work, all her plans, all her dreams...shattered.

That money she'd hoped to win to buy her freedom from her parents was gone. That bud of hope growing inside her for a life away from her parents—gone.

Her life with Silas—gone.

————

JOSEPHINE TOSSED ONLY HER ESSENTIALS ON THE FLOORBOARDS OF

her truck. Chet had agreed to load up Comet, and the rest of her gear, and take Cora home after the rodeo.

She couldn't stay. Not after she'd ruined everything.

Besides the thought of saying goodbye to Silas left a gaping wound where her heart should be. She'd thought the tears would flow and never stop, but her eyes were dry, as if the rest of her body had shut down along with her heart.

Cora came up behind her. Even beneath the heavy makeup, her friend had gone pale. She hadn't told Cora she was leaving. She hadn't wanted to be talked out of it.

"Cora...what's wrong? Are you okay?"

"I'm fine. I was coming to ask you the same thing."

"I'm...I'm okay. Look, I didn't know how to—"

Cora placed her hand on Josephine's forearm. "You haven't heard, have you?"

"Toby? Did something happen—"

"Sit," Cora said.

Oh crap. Josephine leaned against the side of her truck, the heel of her boot tap, tap, tapping against the ground. "Say it." She pushed the words out with lungs that felt too small.

Cora wrung her hands. "Silas drew Thrasher."

"*W-What?* He refused to ride, right?" But even as Josephine said it, she knew it wasn't true. Not just because this was Cheyenne, but because that was the kind of man Silas was. He didn't give in, and he didn't give up.

He hadn't given up on her, and he certainly wouldn't do it with fifteen hundred pounds of hide and horn and hate.

Cora shook her head. "He's riding."

Josephine sprinted back to the arena. At the chutes, she pushed her way through the other bull riders as they readied for their go. But there was no sign of Silas.

By one of the empty chutes, she spotted Monte and Chet and hurried over to them. "Anyone seen Silas?"

Monte dug his bells out of his bag and jerked his head toward the last chute. "Better hurry if you want to talk to him. He's up in two."

She grabbed the rail and was about to climb over, it was the quickest way to get to Silas, but Chet caught her arm. "He'll be okay. If anyone can ride that bull, it would be him."

Yeah. That's what Silas had said about Toby right before Thrasher put Toby in the hospital. She climbed over three sets of stock panels before she got to Silas.

Thrasher was already in the chute. The stench of urine and manure tainted the air, the bull bellowing and pawing the dirt. The crowd roared as a gate opened and spit out a bull rider a couple chutes down.

"Silas." He didn't turn. He hadn't heard her over the noise. She tapped him on the shoulder.

He turned and his features softened. He didn't have to say anything. Holding out his arms, she stepped into them and wrapped her arms around his waist. Warm and solid and safe.

She wanted this. For life.

The tears threatened, but by sheer force of will, she held them back. The last thing she wanted to do was upset him. She could keep it together for him. She had to.

With a finger under her chin, he lifted her face to his and lowered his lips to hers. The kiss tender, not demanding.

Love not lust.

He swayed and caught himself on the rail.

She leaned back so she could get a better look at him. "You okay?"

"Just drunk on love."

He'll never give up. The noise died down, and Josephine knew she had to ask. Knew what his answer would be even before the words left her mouth. "Don't do this. Don't ride him."

"Foss," a guy from the chutes called out. "You're up."

Brushing a thumb across her cheek, he said, "I gotta go."

He didn't wait for her response. Hand over hand he climbed over the rail, settling his legs on either side of the chute, the bull raking the rails with his thick horns. Glancing back at her, he tossed her a cocky smile and gave her a wink and straddled the bull.

He'll be fine. He'll be fine. He'll be fine.

But what if he wasn't?

"Wait!" She scrambled up the chute.

"Hey, lady," one of the guys said, "You can't be here."

"Silas."

He glanced up as someone tried to pull her off the rails, but she held on tight. "I love you."

He shook his head and laughed.

"Why's that funny?"

"Now I know I'm going to die."

"Don't say that. You're not going to die."

"No hotstuff, I'm not."

Even though they were over, she'd be devastated if he were maimed or killed. "Don't do this." She hated to beg, but she would when the man she loves' life was at stake.

"I gotta. For Toby." He gave her a wink that froze the breath in her tight lungs.

She nodded once, her throat too tight to speak.

The smile slid from his lips as he worked the tail end of the rope around his hand and settled on top of the bull. He gave a quick, tight nod and the chute opened.

———

She loves me.

For the first time since he'd climbed on the back of a bull as a lanky kid, the adrenaline that hit him had absolutely nothing to do with the upcoming ride. His vision cleared, his constant headache dulled, and the thump of his heart in his chest beat for one reason.

Josephine.

But he had a job to do, and a bull's rideless record to break.

Silas gave a quick, tight nod and the chute opened.

For once he had no sense of time, his internal clock never started. All he saw was the blur of the stands, the shouting and clapping and stomping was so loud it shocked his eardrums into silence. Thrasher spun to the left then spun to the right, then twisted and turned. Silas held on as if his life depended on it, and in this case, with this bull, it did.

He wasn't going home in a body bag. He was going home with Josephine.

The sound of the buzzer came quick. He freed his hand and jumped clear of the bull.

Silas's feet hit the ground and he sunk to his knees, the eruption of cheers from the stands drowning out all other sound.

He'd done it.

He'd ridden an unrideable bull.

As he went to get up, he stumbled. One of the gateman ran over and helped him to safely to the chutes while the bullfighters dealt with the bull. He climbed over and almost fell to his knees on the other side. The other bull riders thumped him on his back, congratulating him. They thought he was overwhelmed with emotion, but something was wrong. Very wrong.

Someone found a folding chair and dumped him in it, but all he wanted to do was find Josephine. He grabbed onto the rails, his legs steadier now, despite the relentless pounding in his head.

He hadn't made it five steps from the chute area when a reporter, a camera guy, and Maynard rushed toward him.

"Silas," the reporter said, "How's it feel to be the first one to ride Thrasher to the buzzer, and with a personal best score to boot?"

He hadn't seen the score. Personal best? Hot damn.

Another reporter showed up, with another cameraman. Maynard wedged himself beside Silas as if he were the one who'd beaten the beast.

The interviews dragged on and on. He and Josephine were supposed to meet after his ride. He didn't have the time or the patience for all the publicity and chatter. He tried to excuse himself, but Maynard caught a hand on his shoulder and whispered in his ear. "You stay until they're finished, or you never ride in one of my rodeo's again."

He wanted to tell Maynard to go screw himself, but they both knew that he couldn't do that. If he won the night, that check would go a long way to putting money down on a pretty piece of land. But it wouldn't be enough.

Silas had to wonder if it would ever be.

———

AFTER THE INTERVIEWS, SILAS HAD TO HANG AROUND BECAUSE AS it turned out, his personal best was enough to win the buckle and the fat check. From one of the other bull rider's with a barrel racer girlfriend, he'd heard about Josephine's five-second penalty.

Why hadn't she said anything before?

Maybe because you were about to go on a suicide ride?

She had to have been devastated, but she still should have told him.

For that matter, where the hell was she? Was she avoiding him?

I love you.

No. Josephine wasn't avoiding him. Those three little words

hadn't been his mind playing tricks. She'd said them to him. He had witnesses.

He stormed through the barn, making a beeline for Comet's stall. If she were anywhere, it would be there.

Down the aisles, he had to dodge ropers, barrel racers, and bulldoggers as they gathered their gear and loaded their horses.

Comet's stall door was open, and the horse lifted his head from his hay net when Silas walked in. Josephine wasn't in the stall, but she had to be close, you didn't just leave a horse tied in a stall with the door open.

He settled on her tack locker in front of her stall to wait her out. The lazy munching and grinding of hay as Comet ate, lulled him. He must have dozed off, because he woke when Chet tapped the locker with the toe of his boot.

"If you're waiting for Josephine, she's not here," Chet said.

Silas fought to open his eyes. He adjusted his hat to cut the glare of the harsh barn lights. "Where is she."

"Gone."

Gone. Silas stood, and Chet tossed Comet's grooming bucket and bridle into the tack locker. Silas tried to digest the meaning of the word, but he didn't know if the word was incomprehensible or if his brain was muddied from his nap.

"What does that mean?" Silas sounded simple and slow minded, and he still had a slight slur.

Chet untied the hay net. Comet strained on the end of his lead rope, his lips extended to pull one last bite of hay out of the net. Chet hitched it over his shoulder and tossed it on top of the locker. "Gone. As in left. As in she went home."

"And you didn't try to stop her?"

"That's not my job." Chet grabbed a manure fork and wheelbarrow and started mucking out Comet's stall.

Why would Josephine leave? Silas paced to the next stall and back again. They had plans to meet after. They were going to talk and make things right.

But she'd never promised.

Silas pinched the bridge of his nose, but it did nothing to stave off an impending migraine. "Tell me exactly what she said."

Chet leaned against the manure fork with both hands. "She said 'take care of Comet, I'm going home.'"

"That's it?"

"Yeah, man. That's it." With a shrug, Chet went back to mucking. He scooped a pile, shook out the shavings, then dumped the manure into the wheelbarrow. "Do you want my advice?"

Fuck. He couldn't believe he was going to say this. "Yes."

"Let her go. You had your fun. Now it's over."

"You're just saying that because you want her for yourself."

"Says the man who wants her for *himself.*" A guess, but from the pinched expression on Chet's face, not a wild one.

"Doesn't matter what I want," Chet said. Silas gave him points for honesty. "It only matters what *she* wants. Apparently, that's not you."

"She loves me." Silas laughed at himself, knowing how desperate, how pathetic, it made him sound.

"Not enough to stay." Chet set the manure fork aside and picked up the handles of the full wheelbarrow. "I've got work to do."

Silas blocked Chet's path out of the stall. "Give me her number."

"Cox won't want you calling."

"Let me worry about Cox."

It was like pulling teeth out of a saber-toothed tiger, but Silas got the number from a begrudging Chet. Silas scrounged through Josephine's locker, found a pen and an old envelope, and wrote the number down. He didn't trust something that important to his memory.

On his way out of the barn, he passed by Chet as the man dumped the manure into the bucket of a front-end loader. "Take good care of Comet."

Chet sighed. Silas had that coming. "*That* is my job. I know how to do it."

Back at his camper, Silas packed his gear with practiced efficiency. Which pretty much meant he threw his rig bag on the bed, made sure there were no bottles or other breakables that would roll off the counters, and locked the back of the camper.

Everything in his body screamed for him to head south to Texas and Josephine, but he headed west instead, back to Salinas, back to Toby. It wasn't that he was giving up on Josephine.

That would *never* happen.

But he couldn't leave Toby hanging. Silas had to see with his own eyes that Toby was okay, then he could throw himself one hundred percent into winning Josephine over.

But before that, he had a number to call and a winning check to cash.

———

THE ENDLESS RIBBON OF HIGHWAY STRETCHED OUT IN FRONT OF HIS windshield, a monotonous series of headlights and small towns, and a bag full of more cash than he'd ever seen in his entire life beside him.

Despite almost nodding off a couple of times, he only stopped for gas and coffee and to take a piss. Not necessarily in that order.

He slipped his sunglasses on his face, even though it had been dark for hours, but the headlights and streetlights through the towns blinded him and sent pain shooting to the back of his eyes. The sunglasses helped. Some.

Sometime before dawn, he pulled into the parking lot of Toby's hospital in Salinas. He poured himself out of the truck, catching his balance on stiff, creaky, legs. He took a step and stretched his arms over his head, then a blinding, searing, brain-melting pain erupted behind his eyes. A strangled cry ripped from his throat as the pain encompassed his entire head. His stomach roiled, and he latched onto his truck's side mirror to keep from falling to his knees.

His stomach heaved again, and he tossed up the last two pots of coffee he'd used as fuel on the drive down. He pulled himself to his feet, his legs wobbly, his stomach unsettled. Toward the emergency room doors, he staggered. The doors swished open automatically, and he stumbled through.

He lurched to the reception desk, looking for a trash can in case his stomach revolted again. "I'm here t—"

Pain, hot, excruciating clamped down on his head. He pressed the heels of his hands against his eye sockets to hold the agony at bay. "I'm here to see—"

Then his vision went black, his legs buckled, and the floor sucker punched him in the face.

———

Since she'd been back home, Josephine had looked forward each day to getting her mother on Comet. It was the closest she'd been to riding since Cheyenne.

Each day her mother was getting stronger, thanks to Comet. At first, her mother couldn't stay in the saddle without Chet on one side of the horse and Josephine on the other, each with a hand on her mother's hip, keeping her centered, and even then, it was only for a few minutes at a time. Now her mother could stay in the saddle by herself and had worked her time in the saddle up to thirty minutes or more.

With infinite patience, Comet stood beside the mounting platform Chet had built so Josephine's mother could climb into the saddle. It was still slow going getting her mother to grip the horn and lift her leg over the cantle of the big western saddle. When her mother was situated, Josephine fed her mother's feet into the stirrups and led Comet out of the arena and past the big red barn.

"You sure this is a good idea?" Her mother looked closer to sixty than her forty-five years. The skin around her neck sagged from the rapid loss of weight, and her muscle tone had deteriorated to the point where walking and doing for herself, though improving, was a daily struggle.

Josephine stopped and glanced back at her mother. "We can stay in the arena if you want, but aren't you tired of walking in circles? Comet won't take a wrong step, I promise you."

Today they were going to push her mother's endurance a little farther and head out to the pond. There were gentle ups and downs and uneven terrain along the way, but Josephine knew her mother could do it, and Comet could use the exercise himself. Josephine had little hope of being able to leave for the fall circuit, but if by some miracle she could, they'd never win if Comet lost all his condition.

Josephine led Comet for her mother. It took them twenty minutes to get to the pond, a ride that should have taken ten at a normal walk. Comet dipped his toes in the water and leaned down for a drink. He hadn't broken a sweat, but late August in the Texas Hill Country was hot, even when the morning sun wasn't high.

"Monte Shaw called this morning," her mother said. "He thought maybe you would want to go to the diner for lunch tomorrow."

"*Mooom*," Josephine warned. "I'm not going out with Monte Shaw. We've been over this. Why is he calling and talking to you instead of me anyway? Who does that?"

"Probably because you won't take his calls. I don't see why you won't go. He's a decent enough man, and you could do a whole lot worse than—"

"Decent enough? Since when has a Shaw *ever* been decent enough for this family?" Josephine's pitch climbed with her incredulity. "Do you hear yourself?"

Her mother didn't say anything. Comet twitched an ear in her direction, but otherwise kept munching on the weeds along the pond's shoreline. "And even if there wasn't that inane feud between Dad and Monte's father, I'm not settling for *decent enough*."

Not when she'd had much better.

Not when she'd had Silas.

But she'd blown that.

Even if Silas could ever forgive her for running out on him, even if she wanted to apologize, she had no way of getting in touch with him. She didn't have his number, and she hadn't been able to find it through information, and yeah, she'd called. More than once.

"At this point, you should consider yourself lucky that Monte is even interested."

"What are you saying, mother? Just because I'm not a virgin anymore doesn't make me a leper. This isn't the eighteen hundreds."

"Don't talk like that. Against our better judgment, we let you go. You sowed your oats. You went out in the world and got that nonsense out of your system. We supported—"

"Whoa," Josephine said it with enough force that Comet froze mid graze. She scratched him on the shoulder, and he went back to his snack. "I supported *myself*. You and dad gave me nothing, not a penny, not even a blessing."

"We sent Chet."

"I didn't need a spy."

"He wasn't a spy."

Josephine let her arms flop at her sides. "Fine. A babysitter then."

"Well, you can't waste your life on a bull rider. You're better than that."

"Monte rides bulls, Mom. Or hadn't you noticed."

"But his family has money. When he inherits his father's land—"

Josephine huffed out a bitter laugh. "I can't believe you just said that. So this is about money, about dad expanding the ranch. Not about my happiness. *You* married a bull rider. One with no money. Or have you conveniently forgotten that part?" She held her arms out indicating the whole ranch. "Seemed to have worked out for you."

"That's different."

"No, mom. It's not."

"T-They'll break your heart." Her mother settled her hat lower on her head. Tears didn't fall, but Josephine suspected they were close. Sometimes her mother was a hard woman to love, but Josephine loved her anyway.

"Mom," Josephine stepped closer and rubbed her hand on her mother's leg, softening her voice. "What are you talking about?"

"Never mind." Her mother sniffed and sat up straighter. "It was a long time ago. I'm tired. Take me back."

Her mother gave Comet's reins a light tug even though Josephine had control with the lead rope. Josephine clucked to him, and Comet took one last bite before following.

On the walk back, Josephine's thoughts spun with what her

mother had alluded to. Had her father cheated? Worse? But when she looked over her shoulder to ask more questions, her mother had that firm set to her lips and that far off look she sometimes got in her eye. Josephine wouldn't be getting any answers today, and most likely, ever.

"How about Chet," Josephine said, more as a joke as anything else. Even though she'd known him all her life, sometimes she got the impression he might have feelings for her.

"That's not even funny." Her mother's voice was cold enough to refreeze the polar ice caps and relaunch a new ice age. "Did that man ever touch—"

"No, Mom. He's never touched me." Her mother's demeanor sent a ripple up Josephine's spine. "He wouldn't. Dad treats him like a son."

The way her mother's mouth screwed up and her lip curled, her mother would have spit if she were less of a lady. Josephine turned back around. They didn't talk the rest of the way back.

When they returned to the arena, Chet helped her mother off the horse, but the proud woman refused help back to the house. Instead, insisting on using her walker instead of the wheelchair that Chet had brought out for her.

"I'll cool him out," Chet said, talking about Comet.

"Thanks for the offer, but I've got him."

"Fair enough." Chet headed to the barn.

When he'd made it to the arena gate, she asked something she'd always wanted to know. "Chet?"

He stopped and turned.

"Did Silas really come looking for me after the rodeo?"

He released the gate lever and returned to her. "He did."

"Okay." Her gut caved, feeling like she'd come out on the losing end of a knockout round of boxing. Even though her throat had gone tight, she still had more to say and forced the words out, not caring that her voice would tremble or that she would sound a little desperate. She was. No point in hiding the truth. "I really miss him."

Chet removed his hat and wiped the sweat from his brow looking as if he'd rather be anywhere else but there. "Look, I never told you this, but that night after the rodeo, he asked for your number. It's been over a month. Don't you think if he'd been serious, he'd have called you?" Chet took a step closer, his calloused thumb brushing a lazy trail down her cheek. "I would have."

What? His gaze grew dark, serious, and she saw something there she'd never seen before. "What are you doing?"

"Nothing." Chet dropped his hand and took a step back. "Forget him, Josephine. Trust me, if you'd meant anything at all to him, he would have called."

Which only made Josephine wonder, had Silas called? Would her mother or father have told her if he had? Her stomach went wonky as if it didn't know if it should drop with dread or slap a high-five of hope.

She didn't know, but she was about to find out.

After putting Comet in the large pasture with his buddies, and seeing to a few more chores, Josephine went to find her father. Up near the house, she found her father's coverall covered legs sticking out from beneath one of the trucks they used to haul the horse trailers.

"Dad?"

She heard the slap of a wrench against metal, a grunt and a muttered curse. "Shouldn't you be fixing your mother lunch?"

"It's barely noon, and she had a late breakfast. She can survive a few—"

"*Josephine Waylon Cox.*" It seemed like she hadn't gone a day in the last month without one of her parents using her full name. She wasn't ten anymore, but sometimes she felt like it.

Ok, so using the word *survive* in the same sentence as her

mother so soon after her stroke, probably wasn't the best choice of words. "Sorry, Dad. That's not what I meant."

Her father scooted out from beneath the truck and stood, wiping his greasy hands and a bloodied knuckle on a rag he'd snatched from his back pocket. "You shouldn't leave your mother alone, she—"

"She's fine, Dad. She's stronger every day. She's getting around on her own, she can bathe herself, eat by herself. She doesn't need someone hovering over her every second of every day."

"If this is about the fall circuit, I've already made up my mind, and the answer is no."

This wasn't about the circuit. It was about something much more important to her future. "Has Silas called for me?"

"Who?" Her father buried his head under the hood and started fiddling with the carburetor.

"Silas Foss. He called, didn't he?" As soon as the words were out of her mouth, she had no doubt they were true. She didn't even give her father time to deny it. "When? When did he call?"

Her father looked up at her. There was no remorse in his eyes. "Turn the key, would you?"

"What? No. Answer the question."

Her father shouldered past her and climbed into the driver's seat, but before he could turn the key in the ignition, she reached into the open window and yanked out the keys.

"Tell me when he called, or so help me, I'll toss your keys so far into the hay field you'll never find them."

"Caine Cox's only daughter is not hooking up with a no-account bull rider."

"This isn't about you or what you want. I love him."

"You're a kid. You don't—"

"No, Dad. I'm not your little girl anymore. I'm a grown

woman who loves a damn fine man. I have a mind of my own, with hopes, plans, dreams, desires."

Her father turned green at the mention of desires and stared out the windshield, as if she would relent if he ignored her long enough.

She brought her arm back, ready to pitch the keys as far as she could throw them. "Last chance. *When?*"

"That Sunday. After the Cheyenne rodeo. You were already on your way home."

Josephine dropped the keys in the dirt at her feet. "You should have told me."

"You had more important things to worry about. You had your mother to take care of and—"

"Don't use mother as an excuse to keep me from Silas. I'm here. I'm doing my duty. You had no right to mess with my life." Her pulse pounded at her temple. She wanted to yell and scream and holler. More than that, the impulse to load Comet into her trailer and head down the road and never look back, hit hard.

She turned on her heel, determined to do just that.

She'd made it only a few steps before the truck door slammed behind her, and her father said, "Before you storm off, there's one more thing you should know."

Though she stopped, she didn't turn to face him. She couldn't bear to look at him right now. Her father was supposed to protect her, not betray her.

"The night he called, I wired Foss twenty thousand dollars to stay away. He hasn't called since. How's that for a *damn fine* man?"

14

———————

As Silas drove under the arched Rockin' C sign, he slipped on his shades. The sun setting over the harsh scrabble of the Hill Country flashed in his eyes. Bright lights and the sun still hurt, but after nearly two months, he no longer had to reach for the pills to relieve the pain.

Silas didn't drive fast, and he didn't drive slow down the gravel road to Caine Cox's ranch. His belly did a slow roll, as much from hunger as nerves. It had been two, long, excruciating months since Josephine had said she loved him.

He'd almost called again, many, many times. Toby had told him he was an idiot not to, but he'd been at a loss for words. How do you tell the woman that you love that you almost died?

That's not something you tell someone over the phone.

If he had called, if she hadn't come, it would have killed him. Not that he'd wanted her to see him laid flat out in the hospital, helpless like that anyway.

She may not want anything to do with him, but if she didn't, he was going to make her say it to his face.

Plus, he had unfinished business with her father.

He pulled up to the ranch house, a cozy one-story number

160

wrapped with a porch. Pulling the rear-view mirror toward him, he rubbed his hand over the new patch of hair growing in and covering the two-inch semicircular scar just in front of his right ear. He stuck his hat on his head and climbed out. No one needed to see that, especially not Josephine.

A screen door slammed on the back side of the house, and a man stepped onto the porch, with a shotgun in his hand. Silas was mostly sure Caine Cox's threats had been idle, but...

Silas reached into his truck and pulled out a backpack and waited at the front of his truck. He'd been out of the hospital for a month, and every ounce of weight and strength he'd gained since had been a battle. Leaning a hip against the hood, he let Cox come to him.

"Silas Foss, I assume."

Silas nodded.

"Didn't expect to ever see you here." Cox rested the barrel of his shotgun on his shoulder.

"I told you I would come. Where is she?"

"We had a deal. You got your money. Now leave."

Silas unzipped the backpack and held it open for Cox to see the short stacks of hundred-dollar bills. All in their original little paper wrappers. As pristine as the day he'd picked the money up. He'd almost refused to pick up the money that fateful day, but that would have deprived him of seeing the look on Cox's face when he threw the money back at him.

Silas dropped the bag at Cox's feet. "I can live without roughstock. I can live without the money. I'm not living without Josephine. I love her."

"So you've said before."

Cox was a hard man to impress. Not that Silas needed Cox's approval, but he was smart enough to know life would be a hell of a lot easier with Cox's blessing because despite the friction between Josephine and Cox, he knew she loved her father, and Silas didn't want to get between them.

Cox glared and shifted his weight. Silas didn't know if Cox was going to punch him or shoot him or—

"Silas?" Josephine called out from the front of the barn.

Like an idiot, he raised a hand to wave. Jesus, you would think the doctors had sucked out all his brain cells when they'd gone in and drained all the blood. She took a step and then another. Like at the beginning of rehab, his legs refused to move.

In his mind, he'd pictured her running up to him, and like they do in those sappy movies, he'd wrap her in a hug and swing her around. But she wasn't running. In fact, she turned and went back into the barn.

Cox kicked at the bag of money. "It's not too late. I'll double it if you leave now."

Silas got in Cox's face. Pound for pound, inch for inch, they were well matched, except for Cox's age and Silas's slow recovery. "And you wonder why your daughter fights to stay away from you. You are a sad man, Cox. Josephine's happiness, Josephine's *life*, is not something you can barter with."

"You're not good enough for her. You never will be."

"I won't argue with you there. Lord knows what she sees in me. But whether or not she wants to be with me is her decision, not yours."

———

HE WAS THERE. JOSEPHINE'S THROAT CLOSED, AND HER EYES welled. Had he come back for her or had he come to cut her free? She should have known Silas wasn't the kind of man who would walk away without some sort of closure.

She ducked back in the barn and stared at her partially packed tack locker. The lock had gotten rusty, and the green paint was starting to chip. What was she going to do if Silas had come to tell her it was over?

Or worse, what if her father shot him?

That shotgun had just been for intimidation, right? The proverbial father? Shit. She spun on her heel and ran smack into Silas's chest. He caught her arms and kept her from stumbling.

She opened her mouth to speak, as his lips came down on hers. Not halting and tender and sweet, but demanding and needy and dark, his mood matching her own.

His tongue slid into her mouth, exploring. Hauntingly the same, but intensely different. As he held her to him, taking the kiss deeper, her hands went around his neck. She took the hat off his head and tossed it in her locker, her hand brushing against a patch of short hair on the side of his head.

He stilled, then pulled back.

"What happened to your hair? You fall asleep with gum in your mouth and—" He turned his head and let her see the cropped hair, the angry scar. Her hands went to her mouth. "Silas?"

He reached down and retrieved his hat and plopped it on his head. "I was going to tell you about that."

"When?"

All that tingling at her core from his kisses vanished, and her blood heated in her veins. She crossed her arms over her chest. "I'm sick and tired of the men in my life thinking I'm some innocent kid that they have to protect from the big, bad world. You have a lot of explaining to do, and probably a bit of groveling as well."

He took her hand and closed the lid of her tack locker and sat her down beside him. Removing his hat, Silas scrubbed his hand over the patch of short hair. "I won." He smiled, but it was one of those equivocal ones that said that was the good news right before he delivered the bad. "But I had a brain bleed—"

Brain bleed? "What?" She'd heard the word, but it sat there in her mind as if it had no meaning.

"I had been having headaches that last week or so. I thought it was residual from the concussion, but apparently, I had a slow bleed in my head. Long story short, they caught it... and fixed it."

In his hesitation, she heard the words *in time.* As if he'd been almost out of it.

Josephine couldn't catch her breath. She ran her fingers over his jaw and down his neck to the pulse that pounded near his collarbone.

He looked away and took a deep breath, then met her gaze. "I'm not going to lie. It was a close call."

"Why didn't you call me or have Toby call me? Don't you think I had a right to know?"

She tried to pull her hand out of his, but he wouldn't let her. "I was out for a week, and then...you're the one who left, Josephine." His tone was direct, not accusing.

Her growing anger diffused.

"I didn't call because I didn't know if there was an us."

This was her fault. If she hadn't run, if they'd talked...but as that third can had dropped, her world had shattered. It wasn't because she hadn't won in Cheyenne, it was because she couldn't see where she and Silas could have any kind of future. But she'd grown up a lot in these past two months, and if there was anything in her life that she would do over if she could, it was climbing in that truck and driving back to Texas.

"And then," he said, "the doctors weren't sure what kind of recovery I would have, or if there'd be any permanent damage. With what you were going through with your mother, I didn't want you burdened with that."

"If it had been me in that hospital bed, with the chance of not being a hundred percent, of not being me when I was released, would you have loved me any less?"

"What? No. That's crazy. I love you."

"Yet you think my love is conditional?"

"You told me you loved me. Then you disappeared. What was I supposed to think?"

Her throat spasmed, and she choked back a sob. "I-I'm sorry. I-I—" How could she explain what an idiot she'd been?

"Hey, hey, hey." He pulled her onto his lap and settled her head against his chest. She could hear the steady *rump-tump, rump-tump* of his heart and she concentrated on that. "No apologies. What matters is that I'm here now. We can figure out the rest."

She settled into him, but there was a tension in his body that wouldn't ease. There was something he wasn't telling her.

"Tell me the rest." Her words came out stronger. She and Silas were in this together. Whatever they had to face, at least they had each other.

His hold on her got tighter as if he expected her to run for the hills once he said what he had to say. "I'm broke. The money Toby and I had saved to buy our own land, and the money from my win in Cheyenne, we used it all to pay the hospital bills. And to top it off, the doctors said I can't ride anymore. So not only am I broke, I have no job, and I have no prospects."

"You have me." The money she didn't care about. Silas was a good man. He'd find work, she had no doubt. She had him, and that was all that mattered.

———

"There you are."

Silas shifted in front of his bed in the hayloft of Cox's barn so Josephine wouldn't see what he was up to. Without glancing back, he said, "Wait downstairs, I'll be there in a sec."

But her steps came closer instead of going away. Silas

glanced over his shoulder, then dropped what he had in his hand and turned. She stood in the shaft of light from a set of windows carved into the upper walls of the loft, and he was thankful the light no longer brought him pain.

Her hat sat on her head, her pressed western shirt and jeans hugged her form, and her polished boots shone like new pennies. His breath caught, and he knew that no matter how many times he looked at this woman, her beauty would always hit him hard and fast.

She walked into his arms, and he buried his face into the crook of her neck, breathing in the scent of hay and horses, and that signature salty-sweet mixture that came from within that made her not only the incredible woman that she was, but a force to be reckoned with.

"You all packed?" He rubbed a thumb across her cheek wanting to memorize the softness of her skin.

"Just need to load Comet and pick up Cora. But I have an hour before I have to hit the road."

"I'm going to miss you." When she left, she'd take a piece of his heart, and he had no words to describe the crater it was going to leave in his chest.

She hugged him tight and said the words he wanted, no, *needed*, to hear. "I don't have to go."

But just because he needed to hear them didn't mean he agreed. "Yeah, hotstuff, you do. The fall season is only a few months long, and with Toby coming and working here until the spring, I'll be able to slip away when the circuit swings close and see you ride."

"What about you and my dad?"

"We've come to an understanding this past month or so." Which basically amounted to Cox reluctantly agreeing to give him and Toby room and board, and to teach them the ropes of roughstock ranching, in exchange for free labor. With the tiny caveat that if Silas broke Josephine's heart, her father would kill him.

Seemed fair.

But he had no plans to hurt her, so Silas considered himself relatively safe.

"And my mom?"

"You let us guys worry about her. Besides, she'll hardly let us help her anymore."

With a finger, he lifted her chin so he could see her eyes. "Don't worry. Just relax and ride. That's all you have to do. I'll be here when you get back."

He bent his head and kissed her, not knowing how he was going to get through the next few months without her and not go crazy. He almost wished Cox was sending Chet out on the circuit again to keep an eye on her, but at the same time, the ugly green, jealous part of him was damn glad Chet wasn't going to be around her.

She broke the kiss. "You know, we do have an hour to kill." She took his hand and turned toward his bed. "What's all this?"

On the bed sat a small square box and some wrapping paper. She'd interrupted him before he'd had a chance to finish. "You spoiled the surprise."

"Oooh. What is it, what is it? I love surprises!" Her eyes lit up, and for the bazillionth time, he was struck by how incredibly lucky he was to have her in his life.

"Close your eyes." He had wanted to watch her unwrap his gift, but this would have to do.

Closing her eyes, she held out her hands. Silas reached for her belt buckle, and she smiled. "If I'd known it would be that kind of gift, I'd have put on my fancy underwear."

"Sadly, it's not that kind of gift." He chuckled, and it took all he had to stop at only removing her belt.

"Hurry," she said, as he removed her buckle from her belt, and attached the silver and gold one he'd won in Cheyenne.

He re-buckled her belt at her waist and gave it a little tug as he pulled her closer. "You can look now."

She glanced down at the buckle and ran her finger over the raised gold lettering. "Oh my god. I can't take your buckle. This is yours, this is—"

He pressed a finger to her lips. "I love you, Josephine. I don't have much, but I have you, which makes me the richest man in Texas." In her eyes, he could see her soul and her love. The emotions they raised, made his throat tight, and he had to clear his voice to speak again. "But what I do have is yours. I want you to keep this, to wear this. I wanted to give you a ring, but..." He shrugged. One day. "But until then, I want you to have this. I want everyone to know you're mine and I'm yours. When you get back, if I don't have the money, we're going to melt it down, and I'll have them make you the most amazing ring you've—"

"I don't need a ring, cowboy. All I need is you."

He scooped her up. Her legs wrapped around his waist and he spun her. When he finally put her down, she glanced at her watch, and a saucy smile lifted her lips. He loved that smile. Amazing things happened when she got that smile. Earth shattering, life-changing things. She brushed against his erection. "We still have fifty-three minutes to kill."

He stepped her back until her legs hit the bed and she plopped down onto it. He fell on top of her, brushing the empty box and the wrapping paper onto the floor.

With so little time, he refused to waste any. He stripped them of their clothes in Guinness Book of Records time, his hand coming to rest on the flat of her stomach. He kissed his way from her neck, down between her breasts. Down, down, down to the thatch of hair between her legs. Her breath hitched, and her fingers caught in his hair.

"If my dad catches us—"

He flicked his tongue, and she swallowed her words. The rash of goosebumps that broke out over her body brought a devilish grin to his face. "Don't worry, baby. He hasn't caught us, yet."

Lazy S Ranch
LYRICAL CARESS
VICKI THARP
Cowgirl, Unexpectedly

EXCERPT

COWGIRL, UNEXPECTEDLY (LAZY S RANCH BOOK 1)

Published by Lyrical Caress

Universal Buy Link

Chapter 1

The road is my addiction, an incessant quest, a burning itch I can't quite scratch.

After a year of living on the road, I sometimes wonder if I'll ever find what I'm looking for. I just hope I'll recognize it when I see it.

Last night, I'd slalomed my Harley through Wyoming's windy, mountain roads, challenging my still-healing body. Now my muscles burned in my back and shoulders as I scrounged around in my saddlebags for enough money to cover my bitter coffee and butter-bathed toast from the diner.

Where had the rest of my money gone?

A breeze kicked up and I zipped my grandfather's WWII flight jacket to fend off the post-dawn chill. Off to my right, two pickups pulled up. A late model Ford diesel with all the trimmings and a two-door jalopy with its red paint sunburned away to bare metal, a frayed bungee cord strapping down the hood.

A cowboy in a pressed western shirt and jeans climbed out of the Ford, walked around, and then leaned against the driver's side fender of the older truck. A deep tan told tales of his time out in the sun and his boots had enough scuffing to make me believe they were more than a fashion statement.

He settled his wide-brimmed hat low on his head to cut the glare of the sun. Dirty fingerprints stained the brim, and dried sweat ringed the crown. A teenager climbed down from her truck.

"This isn't gonna work," the man said, before the girl's boots even touched the ground. He didn't raise his voice, but tension arced between them, standing the hair on my arms and stirring Dread in my belly.

Yes, Dread. With a capital D. A salty old bastard of a marine that had claimed squatting rights in the pit of my stomach like it was his own personal foxhole. He'd moved in when I'd deployed overseas. He was mean. He was nasty.

And he'd saved this woman's life a time or two.

He also never got the message he could stand down now that I was back stateside and sometimes spotted trouble where none existed.

"We had an agreement," the girl said. "Figures, you'd want to back out of it now."

I tucked my head and tried to ignore them. Since I've been back, I've tried to stay out of other people's business and keep an eye on my own six.

"This is going to be hard enough without adding conditions," the man said. "Have you considered anyone else's feelings? What about your grandfather? Your grandmother? Don't you think they've been through enough already?"

"So this is all my fault now?" The girl's laughter rang as hollow as a cracked bell. "Perfect. Thank you for that. I knew this meet-up was a bad idea."

At the bottom of my second saddlebag, I found enough dirt-encrusted coins to cover my tab, but somewhere on the road, I must have lost my last two hundred dollars.

Damn.

My skin prickled with heat and itched with the need to sweat like it used to when mortar fire crept closer and closer to the base's blast walls. I sucked in a breath of frigid air and held it until the sting abated.

So, this is it then. The end of the road.

As I stepped toward the diner, the girl yanked open her truck door. The cowboy grabbed her wrist.

"Let. Me. Go," the teenager ground out. "I don't have to talk to you."

The girl didn't struggle, but she notched her chin up. By the tremble in her upper lip, it had taken everything she had to keep her voice from cracking. She was tall and wiry, just shy of gaining curves. A dirty red bandanna hung from the back pocket of her faded jeans, and bailing twine restrained a brunette ponytail. I liked this girl already.

"You're gonna have to talk to me some time," the man said. "Now's as good a time as any, sweetheart." If he'd shouted, I might've gone about my business, but something about his smooth tone and calm demeanor raised my hackles.

"Is there a problem?" I asked him even as my brain told me this wasn't what minding my own business looked like. Further proof I was better off limiting my contact with civilians.

"No problem," they replied in unison.

He let go of the girl and she took a small step back, averting her gaze and kicking at a small pebble with her boot. The man glanced at the name patch on my great grandfather's jacket. "Parish, is it?"

I nodded. "Mackenzie."

The man raised a dark blond brow at me and a cocky smile twitched at the corner of his mouth. Mr. Cowboy topped off at about six-one, so he had a good six inches and sixty pounds of muscle on me—a woman of my size didn't threaten him—but brawn doesn't always win. My ex-boyfriend, if you could've called him that, hadn't felt threatened by me either, but he won't make that mistake again.

Off the top of my head, thanks to Uncle Sam and my combat training, I knew how to neutralize a target with my bare hands.

Only a few of them were survivable.

I fixed my eyes on his, in the way that had made most of the men in my unit squirm. He had the beginnings of crow's feet at the corners of his eyes but his short stubble was free of gray. Maybe thirty-six. Seven years older than me. *Not* that I'm in the market.

He crossed his arms over his chest, unfazed, with a hint of humor in his eye. Not as if he were laughing at me, but as if he'd learned not to take life so seriously sometimes.

I should have apologized. I should've backed off while I had the chance. I didn't—me, people, the combination was *no bueno.* "She's a little young for you, don't you think?"

The girl snickered behind me and he shot her a look over my shoulder that did little to shut her up. His lips flattened, but the amused gleam in his eyes remained as if he were withholding a good punchline. He shrugged one shoulder by way of comment.

"You coming in?" he asked the girl as he hefted himself off the side of her truck.

"I think I lost my appetite." She said it like a challenge, like she was daring him to argue with her. And yet almost like she wanted to join him. He blinked twice as if he could clear his vision enough to see what she was really saying. Then he gave up.

"Suit yourself," he said as he strode into the café without a backward glance.

She climbed into her pickup, and its hinges groaned when she heaved the heavy door closed. I headed inside to pay my bill and she mumbled something to me through her open window.

"What was that?" Glancing over my shoulder, I bit back all the things I wanted to tell her. Things like she had her whole life ahead of her, and that she didn't have to settle for a man who was almost old enough to be her father. Then again I could have read the situation all wrong. It wasn't any of my business.

"Hank." She waved her hand toward the café. "He's really not so bad."

Maybe. Maybe not. I nodded to her then made my way up the steps of the café, wondering how much of an ass I'd made of myself. Inside, the man she'd called Hank sat with his back to me, sharing a table with an older gentleman.

At the front counter, I counted out my change—dimes, nickels, pennies, and the occasional quarter to speed up the process.

A hand landed on my jacketed forearm. I didn't think. I didn't have to. Training kicked in. I grabbed his hand, shoved the man face down against the counter and pinned his left arm behind his back. I released him almost as fast as I'd restrained him, and the rapid *rat-a-tat-tat* of my heart dropped back to normal in the span of a few seconds.

I know I'm not in Iraq. I know everyone isn't out to get me. Sometimes it just takes me a moment to remember that.

A stark reminder I'm not like everyone else. I doubted I would ever be again.

The old man chuckled. Here I thought I was nuts. I lifted my gaze and he stretched his shoulder to relieve the pain from the bind I'd put him in. His pale blue eyes held a thin mixture of amusement and perhaps understanding. I tried for a smile, even though the expression felt foreign on my face.

"Sorry about that."

"Where did you serve?" He asked in a way that made me feel like the crazy train hadn't just left the station.

"Iraq," I said. "Fallujah," to be more specific. Something in his demeanor made me want to add 'sir' to my answer.

He nodded once like a commander to a subordinate, laid a ten-dollar bill on the counter, and pushed it toward the wide-eyed waitress. "For the lady's breakfast," he told her and stuck out his hand to shake mine. "Thank you for your service. Glad you made it back in one piece."

A half laugh escaped me—full of irony and empty of humor. Physically, I was in one piece, more or less. Emotionally? I was shattered. Each shard so minuscule, no way could I ever superglue them back together again, so I'd never really tried.

I didn't want this man's help or his money. However, I accepted it and thanked him anyway.

As weird as it sounds, I felt I owed him that much.

After a modest tip, between the coins I'd found and the change from his ten, I'd have enough for a gallon or two of gas, maybe a tad more. It might get me around the next bend, or perhaps up into the next mountain range, but nowhere near where I wanted to be.

He stepped back to his table. Hank hadn't stirred from his seat. "So much for coming to my rescue," the old man ribbed him.

As I headed out the door, I caught Hank's reply. "Not the first time I've let you down." Then he added, "I doubt it'll be the last." His self-deprecating tone lost its light, shifting to something darker.

*** *

Dense clouds obscured the peaks of the mountains flanking the valley making my location feel like a world of its own. It could be heaven for all I knew, but without my last two hundred dollars, it felt a whole lot more like hell.

I'd known my days on the road were numbered. I just hadn't expected it to be in a no-stop-light town. I needed to earn some money, but this high plain valley wasn't exactly ripe with employment opportunities.

After fueling, I paid for my gas and spotted the "Help Wanted" ad on the crowded bulletin board. "You know anything about this ranch?" I asked the kid who'd rung me up.

He shrugged his narrow shoulders. "Busy time of year. Plus they've had a run of bad luck."

"So the job is temporary?"

"I reckon." He shrugged again. Easy. Automatic. Habit. I tore the ad off the board. It had phone number tabs at the bottom, but I didn't have a cell phone and after paying for the gas, I didn't have money for a pay phone either. If I could even find one.

There was a map to the ranch drawn in the corner. "Mind if I take this?" "Free country."

Yes, it was.

Outside, I swung my leg over my motorcycle. At over seventy years old, the bike showed wear—leg rubs on either side of the faded black tank, pitted chrome, and the edges of the leather seat and saddlebags were alligatored with age. Like an old T-shirt, it molded to my body. It was comfortable. It was familiar. And we'd experienced many of life's difficulties together.

I jumped on the kick-starter and blipped the throttle as the engine roared to life. The rumble and vibration of the bike shook the unease from my nerves as I settled into the seat to memorize the map. The job sounded promising. Hard work had never scared me. I needed the money. It was temporary.

Practically perfect.

Glancing both ways, I pulled in front of a slow-moving tractor, my helmet strapped to the side of the seat behind me. It bumped my leg as I shifted into a higher gear. Before deployment, I never rode without my helmet. Since I've been back, I've worn it less and less. Don't get me wrong, I'm not suicidal. I don't have a death wish.

I'm just not certain it matters much if I die.

*** *

My engine sputtered and stopped on the downhill road into Lazy S Ranch, like an old dinosaur rattling out its last breath. I coasted the rest of the way and skidded to a halt in front of a small group of men gathered around a campfire.

I climbed off and stepped to the edge of the circle of men. My engine ticked as it cooled and thin tendrils of campfire smoke curled into the air, but the handful of hot coals remaining provided little heat.

A sharp whistle from an older man I assumed was the boss or ranch foreman, hushed their chatter, yet all eyes remained on me. Men don't intimidate me, but I swallowed a grumble when my eyes settled on Hank from the café.

One of the cowboys spit on the ground. Another stopped whittling. A kid of about nineteen or twenty on Hank's right sucked in a hard breath. I thought he might choke on his toothpick.

"Morning, boys," I said, unfazed by the welcome. For a moment, silence reigned. Even the cow dog stopped chewing at his fleas. "Looks like I'm just in time."

"I thought the women's knitting circle met on Wednesdays," the kid muttered around the toothpick.

There was the expected quick round of chuckles. Ignoring the comment, I walked over to the foreman and pulled the flyer from my back pocket. "Says here you need hands. I have two, so I'm here to apply."

"You're a woman," the foreman said as if the statement would come as a revelation to me.

I pasted on a bright smile, ran my hand down my ponytail the same deep brown as the horse tied to a nearby tree, and flattened the front of my bomber jacket that all but hid my breasts. "Kind of you to notice."

"We need men. Strong men. With muscle."

I took the flier from his hand and feigned confusion as I pretended to reread the information printed on the sheet. "No, nothing here specifies men only."

"You have to be able to ride."

"I can ride." He probably meant horses, not motorcycles, but he hadn't qualified the type of riding so I didn't consider it an outright lie. Besides, how hard could it be?

"And shoot," the foreman added.

A genuine smile tipped my lips. "Not a problem."

He crossed his arms over his chest, eyes narrowed. "And wrestle calves." The breath I blew out ruffled my bangs. "Never wrestled calves."

Looking around, I tilted my head, indicating the kid with the toothpick, still lanky from a growth spurt. "But I sure as hell can out-wrestle him."

The group of men burst into hoots and guffaws, and one of them piped up, "Aw, c'mon boss, give her a shot, what can it hurt?"

The foreman scrubbed a hand in nearly a week's growth of beard and sighed. "Got no quarters for ladies, here."

After all the things I've done. I don't think I qualify as a lady anymore.

And in all honesty, I felt more comfortable around men than women. "That shouldn't be a problem." I sauntered over to Hank with mustered bravado and jabbed a thumb in his direction. "I'll bunk with Pops."

Hank jerked his chin up as if I'd landed an uppercut. "Pops?"

He had at least ten years on a couple of the other guys, who weren't long out of the schoolyard at best. It wasn't as if he was *old*, old. Just old enough I wouldn't have to tell him more than once I wasn't interested in a high country romance.

In Iraq, the men had learned to leave me be. These guys would, too. In time. But I needed rack time before I had the energy to deal with it. Besides, I figured I'd already pissed Hank off enough this morning that he'd be the least likely one to hit on me.

Hank eyed me with speculation, the brim of his hat shadowing his expression. "You're no spring chicken either."

I ignored him and let the comment slide, as well as the round of juvenile comments from the guys steeped with sexual innuendo. It wasn't anything I hadn't heard before, and the guys weren't meaning any harm, but if my bones didn't ache and the muscle under the scar on my shoulder didn't burn, I might have argued with him.

An ear-piercing whistle from behind me made me jump. The men quieted mid-laugh and a dog sidled up to my leg and leaned against me. I dropped a hand to its head and felt the quick lick of a hot, moist tongue on my palm. I turned and recognized the man I'd restrained this morning and the young girl walking up from the main house.

The girl's smile was a quirky mixture of shy and amused. The man spared me a brief nod before turning his attention to the rest of the men. "Enough of that kind of talk. My wife and granddaughter live here. I expect you to behave like gentlemen, and treat them"—the man looked between his granddaughter and myself before glaring back at them— "and any other women, with respect. If you cannot manage that, then you'd best go now."

The kid with the toothpick stared down at his boots and kicked sand onto the coals, and someone cleared his throat, but nobody bothered to leave. They had a leanness, a sparseness to them that spoke of a life of hard work without much left for excess. They may have been happy enough with a roof over their heads and a meal in their bellies.

The old man from the diner took a spot next to the foreman and introduced himself as Dale Cunningham, the ranch owner. "My wife is Charlotte, but people call her Lottie. This here is my granddaughter, Jenna."

With a negligent wave of his hand, he then introduced the man next to him. "My foreman here is Link Hardy. I expect you to follow his orders as if they came from me. There's been mischief in the past, but that's behind us now. Disloyalty to the brand or stealing from me or mine won't be tolerated."

All the men nodded, as Dale, in turn, caught each of their eyes. I bobbed my head as well. After all, loyalty and following orders came second nature to me.

"Breakfast and dinner will be served at the main house," Dale continued. "There are groceries in the bunkhouses, so lunches are up to you. You have thirty minutes to stow your gear and pack a lunch. Daylight's wasting and we have fences to check, cattle to work, and horses to round up."

Dale turned and headed to the barn without any fanfare. I figured that meant I, as well as the rest of the men, was hired. The men went to grab their gear from their trucks. Two had their own horses in a stock trailer and they headed over to offload them.

The horses' hooves tapped a nervous, deep staccato on the trailer's wooden floorboards as they backed out and steel clanked on steel as the rear door banged against the shaking trailer.

The bunkhouses were downhill from the campfire, so I straddled my bike and coasted down the ranch road after Hank, trying to pry my eyes off the firm curve of his jeans-clad ass.

ABOUT THE AUTHOR

Vicki Tharp makes her home on small acreage in south Texas with her husband and an embarrassing number of pets. When she isn't writing, you can usually find her on the back of her horse—avoiding anything that remotely resembles housework —smelling like fly spray and horse sweat.

Join my newsletter at: http://eepurl.com/croJgz
Join my street team and receive free Advance Reader Copies of my upcoming books at: http://eepurl.com/cWhXbD
You can find my website at: www.VickiTharp.com
I love to hear from readers. You can email me at
Author@VickiTharp.com

Or you can stalk me at:

facebook.com/VickiTharpAuthor

instagram.com/author_Vicki_Tharp

bookbub.com/authors/vicki-tharp

amazon.com/author/vicki_tharp

twitter.com/vwtharp